# R. K. NARAYAN

## TALES FROM MALGUDI

PENGUIN BOOKS

## PENGUIN BOOKS

Published by the Penguin Group. Penguin Books Ltd, 27 Wrights Lane, London w8 5tz, England. Penguin Books USA Inc., 375 Hudson Street, New York, New York 10014, USA. Penguin Books Australia Ltd, Ringwood, Victoria, Australia. Penguin Books Canada Ltd, 10 Alcorn Avenue, Toronto, Ontario, Canada m4v 3b2. Penguin Books (NZ) Ltd, 182–190 Wairau Road, Auckland 10, New Zealand · Penguin Books Ltd, Registered Offices: Harmondsworth, Middlesex, England · 'An Astrologer's Day', 'Lawley Road', 'The Martyr's Corner', 'Selvi' and 'Emden' are taken from *Malgudi Days* and 'House Opposite', 'The Watchman', 'A Career', 'Like the Sun' and 'The Evening Gift' from *Under the Banyan Tree*, published by Penguin Books in 1984 and 1987 respectively. This edition published 1995 · Copyright © R. K. Narayan, 1972, 1975, 1978, 1980, 1981, 1982, 1985. All rights reserved · Typeset by Datix International Limited, Bungay, Suffolk. Printed in England by Clays Ltd, St Ives plc ·
10 9 8 7 6 5 4 3 2 1

# CONTENTS

# An Astrologer's Day

Punctually at midday he opened his bag and spread out his professional equipment, which consisted of a dozen cowrie shells, a square piece of cloth with obscure mystic charts on it, a notebook and a bundle of palmyra writing. His forehead was resplendent with sacred ash and vermilion, and his eyes sparkled with a sharp abnormal gleam which was really an outcome of a continual searching look for customers, but which his simple clients took to be a prophetic light and felt comforted. The power of his eyes was considerably enhanced by their position – placed as they were between the painted forehead and the dark whiskers which streamed down his cheeks: even a half-wit's eyes would sparkle in such a setting. To crown the effect he wound a saffron-coloured turban around his head. This colour scheme never failed. People were attracted to him as bees are attracted to cosmos or dahlia stalks. He sat under the boughs of a spreading tamarind tree which flanked a path running through the Town Hall Park. It was a remarkable place in many ways: a surging crowd was always moving up and down this narrow road morning till night. A variety of trades and occupations was represented all along its way: medicine-sellers, sellers of stolen hardware and junk, magicians and, above all, an auctioneer of cheap cloth, who created enough din all day to attract the whole town. Next to him in vociferousness came a vendor of fried groundnuts, who gave his ware a fancy name each day, calling it Bombay Ice-Cream one day, and on the next Delhi Almond, and on the third Raja's Delicacy, and so on and so forth, and people flocked to him. A considerable portion of this crowd dallied before the astrologer too. The astrologer transacted his business by the light of a flare which crackled and smoked up above the groundnut heap nearby. Half the enchantment of the place was due to the fact that it did not have the benefit of municipal lighting. The place was lit up by shop lights. One or two had hissing gaslights, some had naked flares stuck on poles, some were lit up by old cycle lamps and one or two, like the astrologer's, managed without lights of their own. It was a bewildering criss-cross of light rays and moving shadows. This suited the astrologer very well, for the simple reason that he had not in the least intended to be an astrologer when he began life; and he knew no more of what was going to happen to others than he knew what was going to happen to himself next minute. He was as much a stranger to the stars as were his innocent customers. Yet he said things which pleased and astonished everyone: that was more a matter of study, practice and shrewd guess-work. All the same, it was as much an honest man's labour as any other, and he deserved the wages he carried home at the end of a day.

He had left his village without any previous thought or plan. If he had continued there he would have carried on the work of his forefathers – namely, tilling the land, living, marrying and ripening in his cornfield and ancestral home. But that was not to be. He had to leave home without telling anyone, and he could not rest till he left it behind a couple of hundred miles. To a villager it is a great deal, as if an ocean flowed between.

He had a working analysis of mankind's troubles: marriage, money and the tangles of human ties. Long practice had sharpened his perception. Within five minutes he understood what was wrong. He charged three pies per question and never opened his mouth till the other had spoken for at least ten minutes, which provided him enough stuff for a dozen answers and advices. When he told the person before him, gazing at his palm, 'In many ways you are not getting the fullest results for your efforts,' nine out of ten were disposed to agree with him. Or he questioned: 'Is there any woman in your family, maybe even a distant relative, who is not well disposed towards you?' Or he gave an analysis of character: 'Most of your troubles are due to your nature. How can you be otherwise with Saturn where he is? You have an impetuous nature and a rough exterior.' This endeared him to their hearts immediately, for even the mildest of us loves to think that he has a forbidding exterior.

The nuts-vendor blew out his flare and rose to go home. This was a signal for the astrologer to bundle up too, since it left him in darkness except for a little shaft of green light which strayed in from somewhere and touched the ground before him. He picked up his cowrie shells and paraphernalia and was putting them back into his bag when the green shaft of light was blotted out; he looked up and saw a man standing before him. He sensed a possible client and said. 'You look so careworn. It will do you good to sit down for a while and chat with me.' The other grumbled some vague reply. The astrologer pressed his invitation; whereupon the other thrust his palm under his nose, saying: 'You call yourself an astrologer?' The astrologer felt challenged and said, tilting the other's palm towards the green shaft of light: 'Yours is a nature . . .' 'Oh, stop that,' the other said. 'Tell me something worthwhile . . .'

Our friend felt piqued. 'I charge only three pies per question, and what you get ought to be good enough for your money . . .' At this the other withdrew his arm, took out an anna and flung it out to him, saying, 'I have some questions to ask. If I prove you are bluffing, you must return that anna to me with interest.'

'If you find my answers satisfactory, will you give me five rupees?'

'No.'

'Or will you give me eight annas?'

'All right, provided you give me twice as much if you are wrong,' said the stranger. This pact was accepted after a little further argument. The astrologer sent up a prayer to heaven as the other lit a cheroot. The astrologer caught a glimpse of his face by the match-light. There was a pause as cars hooted on the road, *jutka*-drivers swore at their horses and the babble of the crowd agitated the semi-darkness of the park. The other sat down, sucking his cheroot, puffing out, sat there ruthlessly. The astrologer felt very uncomfortable. 'Here, take your anna back. I am not used to such challenges. It is late for me today . . .' He made preparations to bundle up. The other held his wrist and said, 'You can't get out of it now. You dragged me in while I was passing.' The astrologer shivered in his grip; and his voice shook and became faint. 'Leave me today. I will speak to you tomorrow.' The other thrust his palm in his face and said, 'Challenge is challenge. Go on.' The astrologer proceeded with his throat drying up. 'There is a woman . . .'

'Stop,' said the other. 'I don't want all that. Shall I succeed in my present search or not? Answer this and go. Otherwise I will not let you go till you disgorge all your coins.' The astrologer muttered a few incantations and replied, 'All right. I will speak. But will you give me a rupee if what I say is convincing? Otherwise I will not open my mouth, and you may do what you like.' After a good deal of haggling the other agreed. The astrologer said, 'You were left for dead. Am I right?'

'Ah, tell me more.'

'A knife has passed through you once?' said the astrologer.

'Good fellow!' He bared his chest to show the scar. 'What else?'

'And then you were pushed into a well nearby in the field. You were left for dead.'

'I should have been dead if some passer-by had not chanced to peep into the well,' exclaimed the other, overwhelmed by enthusiasm. 'When shall I get at him?' he asked, clenching his fist.

'In the next world,' answered the astrologer. 'He died four months ago in a far-off town. You will never see any more of him.' The other groaned on hearing it. The astrologer proceeded.

'Guru Nayak –'

'You know my name!' the other said, taken aback.

'As I know all other things. Guru Nayak, listen carefully to what I have to say. Your village is two days' journey due north of this town. Take the next train and be gone. I see once again great danger to your life if you go from home.' He took out a pinch of sacred ash and held it out to him. 'Rub it on your forehead and go home. Never travel southward again, and you will live to be a hundred.'

'Why should I leave home again?' the other said reflectively. 'I was only going away now and then to look for him and to choke out his life if I met him.' He shook his head regretfully. 'He has escaped my hands. I hope at least he died as he deserved.' 'Yes,' said the astrologer. 'He was crushed under a lorry.' The other looked gratified to hear it.

The place was deserted by the time the astrologer picked up his articles and put them into his bag. The green shaft was also gone, leaving the place in darkness and silence. The stranger had gone off into the night, after giving the astrologer a handful of coins.

It was nearly midnight when the astrologer reached home. His wife was waiting for him at the door and demanded an explanation. He flung the coins at her and said, 'Count them. One man gave all that.'

'Twelve and a half annas,' she said, counting. She was overjoyed. 'I can buy some *jaggery* and coconut tomorrow. The child has been asking for sweets for so many days now. I will prepare some nice stuff for her.'

6  'The swine has cheated me! He promised me a rupee,' said

the astrologer. She looked up at him. 'You look worried. What is wrong?'

'Nothing.'

After dinner, sitting on the *pyol*, he told her, 'Do you know a great load is gone from me today? I thought I had the blood of a man on my hands all these years. That was the reason why I ran away from home, settled here and married you. He is alive.'

She gasped. 'You tried to kill!'

'Yes, in our village, when I was a silly youngster. We drank, gambled and quarrelled badly one day – why think of it now? Time to sleep,' he said, yawning, and stretched himself on the *pyol*.

# Lawley Road

The Talkative Man said:

For years people were not aware of the existence of a Municipality in Malgudi. The town was none the worse for it. Diseases, if they started, ran their course and disappeared, for even diseases must end someday. Dust and rubbish were blown away by the wind out of sight; drains ebbed and flowed and generally looked after themselves. The Municipality kept itself in the background, and remained so till the country got its independence on the fifteenth of August 1947. History holds few records of such jubilation as was witnessed on that day from the Himalayas to Cape Comorin. Our Municipal Council caught the inspiration. They swept the streets, cleaned the drains and hoisted flags all over the place. Their hearts warmed up when a procession with flags and music passed through their streets.

The Municipal Chairman looked down benignly from his balcony, muttering, 'We have done our bit for this great occasion.' I believe one or two members of the Council who were with him saw tears in his eyes. He was a man who had done well for himself as a supplier of blankets to the army during the war, later spending a great deal of his gains in securing the chairmanship. That's an epic by itself and does not concern us now. My present story is different. The satisfaction the Chairman now felt was, however, short-lived.

In about a week, when the bunting was torn off, he became quite dispirited. I used to visit him almost every day, trying to make a living out of news-reports to an upcountry paper which paid me two rupees for every inch of published news. Every month I could measure out about ten inches of news in that paper, which was mostly a somewhat idealized account of municipal affairs. This made me a great favourite there. I walked in and out of the Municipal Chairman's office constantly. Now he looked so unhappy that I was forced to ask, 'What is wrong, Mr Chairman?'

'I feel we have not done enough,' he replied.

'Enough of what?' I asked.

'Nothing to mark off the great event.' He sat brooding and then announced, 'Come what may, I am going to do something great!' He called up an Extraordinary Meeting of the Council, and harangued them, and at once they decided to nationalize the names of all the streets and parks, in honour of the birth of independence. They made a start with the park at the Market Square. It used to be called the Coronation Park – whose coronation God alone knew; it might have been the coronation of Victoria or of Asoka. No one bothered about it. Now the old board was uprooted and lay on the lawn, and a brand-new sign stood in its place declaring it henceforth to be Hamara Hindustan Park.

The other transformation, however, could not be so smoothly worked out. Mahatma Gandhi Road was the most sought-after name. Eight different ward councillors were after it. There were six others who wanted to call the roads in front of their houses Nehru Road or Netaji Subash Bose

Road. Tempers were rising and I feared they might come to blows. There came a point when, I believe, the Council just went mad. It decided to give the same name to four different streets. Well, sir, even in the most democratic or patriotic town it is not feasible to have two roads bearing the same name. The result was seen within a fortnight. The town became unrecognizable with new names. Gone were the Market Road, North Road, Chitra Road, Vinayak Mudali Street and so on. In their place appeared the names, repeated in four different places, of all the ministers, deputy ministers and the members of the Congress Working Committee. Of course, it created a lot of hardship – letters went where they were not wanted, people were not able to say where they lived or direct others there. The town became a wilderness with all its landmarks gone.

The Chairman was gratified with his inspired work – but not for long. He became restless again and looked for fresh fields of action.

At the corner of Lawley Extension and Market there used to be a statue. People had got so used to it that they never bothered to ask whose it was or even to look up. It was generally used by the birds as a perch. The Chairman suddenly remembered that it was the statue of Sir Frederick Lawley. The Extension had been named after him. Now it was changed to Gandhi Nagar, and it seemed impossible to keep Lawley's statue there any longer. The Council unanimously resolved to remove it. The Council with the Chairman sallied forth triumphantly next morning and circumambulated the statue. They now realized their mistake. The statue towered twenty feet above them and seemed to arise from a pedestal of molten lead. In their imagination they had thought that a vigorous resolution would be enough to topple down the statue of this satrap, but now they found that it stood with the firmness of a mountain. They realized that Britain, when she was here, had attempted to raise herself on no mean foundation. But it made them only firmer in their resolve. If it was going to mean blasting up that part of the town for the purpose, they would do it. For they unearthed a lot of history about Sir Frederick Lawley. He was a combination of Attila, the Scourge of Europe, and Nadir Shah, with the craftiness of a Machiavelli. He subjugated Indians with the sword and razed to the ground the villages from which he heard the slightest murmur of protest. He never countenanced Indians except when they approached him on their knees.

People dropped their normal occupations and loitered around the statue, wondering how they could have tolerated it for so many years. The gentleman seemed to smile derisively at the nation now, with his arms locked behind and his sword dangling from his belt. There could be no doubt that he must have been the worst tyrant imaginable: the true picture – with breeches and wig and white waistcoat and that hard, determined look – of all that has been hatefully familiar in the British period of Indian history. They shuddered when they thought of the fate of their ancestors who had to bear the tyrannies of this man.

Next the Municipality called for tenders. A dozen contractors sent in their estimates, the lowest standing at fifty thousand rupees, for removing the statue and carting it to the Municipal Office, where they were already worried about the housing of it. The Chairman thought it over and told me, 'Why don't you take it yourself? I will give you the statue free if you do not charge us anything for removing it.' I had thought till then that only my municipal friends were mad, but now I found I could be just as mad as they. I began to calculate the whole affair as a pure investment. Suppose it cost me five thousand rupees to dislodge and move the statue (I knew the contractors were overestimating), and I sold it as metal for six thousand ... About three tons of metal might fetch anything. Or I could probably sell it to the British Museum or Westminster Abbey. I saw myself throwing up the upcountry paper job.

The Council had no difficulty in passing a resolution permitting me to take the statue away. I made elaborate arrangements for the task ... I borrowed money from my father-in-law, promising him a fantastic rate of interest. I recruited a team of fifty coolies to hack the pedestal. I stood over them like a slave-driver and kept shouting instructions. They put down their implements at six in the evening and returned to their attack early next day. They were specially recruited from Koppal, where the men's limbs were hardened by generations of teak-cutting in Mempi Forest.

We hacked for ten days. No doubt we succeeded in chipping the pedestal here and there, but that was all; the statue showed no sign of moving. At this rate I feared I might become bankrupt in a fortnight. I received permission from the District Magistrate to acquire a few sticks of dynamite, cordoned off the area and lighted the fuse. I brought down the knight from his pedestal without injuring any limb. Then it took me three days to reach the house with my booty. It was stretched out on a specially designed carriage drawn by several bullocks. The confusion brought about by my passage along Market Road, the crowd that followed uttering jokes, the incessant shouting and instructions I had to be giving, the blinding heat of the day, Sir F.'s carriage coming to a halt at every inconvenient spot and angle, moving neither forwards nor backwards, holding up the traffic on all sides, and darkness coming on suddenly with the statue nowhere near my home – all this was a nightmare I wish to pass over. I mounted guard over him on the roadside at night. As he lay on his back staring at the stars, I felt sorry for him and said, 'Well, this is what you get for being such a haughty imperialist. It never pays.' In due course, he was safely lodged in my small house. His head and shoulders were in my front hall, and the rest of him stretched out into the street through the doorway. It was an obliging community there at Kabir Lane and nobody minded this obstruction.

The Municipal Council passed a resolution thanking me for my services. I wired this news to my paper, tacking onto it a ten-inch story about the statue. A week later the Chairman came to my house in a state of agitation. I seated him on the chest of the tyrant. He said, 'I have bad news for you. I wish you had not sent up that news item about the statue. See these . . .' He held out a sheaf of telegrams. They were from every kind of historical society in India, all protesting against the removal of the statue. We had all been misled about Sir F. All the present history pertained to a different Lawley of the time of Warren Hastings. This Frederick Lawley (of the statue) was a military governor who had settled down here after the Mutiny. He cleared the jungles and almost built the town of Malgudi. He established here the first cooperative society for the whole of India, and the first canal system by which thousands of acres of land were irrigated from the Sarayu, which had been dissipating itself till then. He established this, he established that, and he died in the great Sarayu floods while attempting to save the lives of villagers living on its banks. He was the first Englishman to advise the British Parliament to involve more and more Indians in all Indian affairs. In one of his despatches he was said to have declared, 'Britain must quit India someday for her own good.'

The Chairman said, 'The government have ordered us to reinstate the statue.' 'Impossible!' I cried. 'This is my statue and I will keep it. I like to collect statues of national heroes.' This heroic sentiment impressed no one. Within a week all the newspapers in the country were full of Sir Frederick Lawley. The public caught the enthusiasm. They paraded in front of my house, shouting slogans. They demanded the statue back. I offered to abandon it if the Municipality at least paid my expenses in bringing it here. The public viewed me as their enemy. 'This man is trying to black-market even a statue,' they remarked. Stung by it, I wrote a placard and hung it on my door: STATUE FOR SALE. TWO AND A HALF

TONS OF EXCELLENT METAL. IDEAL GIFT FOR A PATRIOTIC FRIEND. OFFERS ABOVE TEN THOUSAND WILL BE CONSIDERED. It infuriated them and made them want to kick me, but they had been brought up in a tradition of non-violence and so they picketed my house; they lay across my door in relays holding a flag and shouting slogans. I had sent away my wife and children to the village in order to make room for the statue in my house, and so this picketing did not bother me – only I had to use the back door a great deal. The Municipality sent me a notice of prosecution under the Ancient Monuments Act which I repudiated in suitable terms. We were getting into bewildering legalities – a battle of wits between me and the municipal lawyer. The only nuisance about it was that an abnormal quantity of correspondence developed and choked up an already congested household.

I clung to my statue, secretly despairing how the matter was ever going to end. I longed to be able to stretch myself fully in my own house.

Six months later relief came. The government demanded a report from the Municipality on the question of the statue, and this together with other lapses on the part of the Municipality made them want to know why the existing Council should not be dissolved and re-elections ordered. I called on the Chairman and said, 'You will have to do something grand now. Why not acquire my house as a National Trust?'

'Why should I?' he asked.

'Because,' I said, 'Sir F. is there. You will never be able to cart him to his old place. It'll be a waste of public money.

Why not put him up where he is now? He has stayed in the other place too long. I'm prepared to give you my house for a reasonable price.'

'But our funds don't permit it,' he wailed.

'I'm sure you have enough funds of your own. Why should you depend on the municipal funds? It'll indeed be a grand gesture on your part, unique in India . . .' I suggested he ought to relieve himself of some of his old blanket gains. 'After all . . . how much more you will have to spend if you have to fight another election!' It appealed to him. We arrived at a figure. He was very happy when he saw in the papers a few days later: 'The Chairman of Malgudi Municipality has been able to buy back as a present for the nation the statue of Sir Frederick Lawley. He proposed to install it in a newly acquired property which is shortly to be converted into a park. The Municipal Council have resolved that Kabir Lane shall be changed to Lawley Road.'

# The Martyr's Corner

Just at that turning between Market Road and the lane leading to the chemist's shop he had his establishment. If anyone doesn't like the word 'establishment', he is welcome to say so, because it was actually something of a vision spun out of air. At eight you would not see him, and again at ten you would see nothing, but between eight and ten he arrived, sold his goods and departed.

Those who saw him remarked thus, 'Lucky fellow! He has hardly an hour's work a day and he pockets ten rupees – what graduates are unable to earn! Three hundred rupees a month!' He felt irritated when he heard such glib remarks and said, 'What these folk do not see is that I sit before the oven practically all day frying all this stuff . . .'

He got up when the cock in the next house crowed; sometimes it had a habit of waking up at three in the morning and letting out a shriek. 'Why has the cock lost its normal sleep?' Rama wondered as he awoke, but it was a signal he could not miss. Whether it was three o'clock or four, it was all the same to him. He had to get up and start his day.

At about 8:15 in the evening he arrived with a load of stuff. He looked as if he had four arms, so many things he carried about him. His equipment was the big tray balanced on his head, with its assortment of edibles, a stool stuck in the crook of his arm, a lamp in another hand, a couple of portable legs for mounting his tray. He lit the lamp, a lantern which consumed six pies' worth of kerosene every day, and kept it near at hand, since he did not like to depend only upon electricity, having to guard a lot of loose cash and a variety of miscellaneous articles.

When he set up his tray with the little lamp illuminating his display, even a confirmed dyspeptic could not pass by without throwing a look at it. A heap of *bondas*, which seemed puffed and big but melted in one's mouth; *dosais*, white, round and limp, looking like layers of muslin; *chapattis* so thin that you could lift fifty of them on a little finger; duck's eggs, hard-boiled, resembling a heap of ivory balls; and perpetually boiling coffee on a stove. He had a separate aluminium pot in which he kept chutney, which went gratis with almost every item.

He always arrived in time to catch the cinema crowd coming out after the evening show. A pretender to the throne, a young scraggy fellow, sat on his spot until he arrived and did business, but our friend did not let that bother him unduly. In fact, he felt generous enough to say, 'Let the poor rat do his business when I am not there.' This sentiment was amply respected, and the pretender moved off a minute before the arrival of the prince among caterers.

His customers liked him. They said in admiration, 'Is there another place where you can get coffee for six pies and four *chapattis* for an anna?' They sat around his tray, taking what they wanted. A dozen hands hovered about it every minute, because his customers were entitled to pick up, examine and accept their stuff after proper scrutiny.

Though so many hands were probing the lot, he knew exactly who was taking what: he knew by an extraordinary sense which of the *jutka*-drivers was picking up *chapattis* at a given moment; he could even mention his licence number; he knew that the stained hand nervously coming up was that of the youngster who polished the shoes of passers-by; and he knew exactly at what hour he would see the wrestler's arm searching for the perfect duck's egg, which would be knocked against the tray corner before consumption.

His custom was drawn from the population swarming the pavement: the boot-polish boys, for instance, who wandered to and fro with brush and polish in a bag, endlessly soliciting, 'Polish, sir, polish!' Rama had a soft corner in his heart for the waifs. When he saw some fat customer haggling over the payment to one of these youngsters he felt like shouting, 'Give the poor fellow a little more. Don't grudge it. If you pay an anna more he can have a *dosai* and a *chapatti*. As it is, the poor fellow is on half-rations and remains half-starved all day.'

It rent his heart to see their hungry, hollow eyes; it pained him to note the rags they wore; and it made him very unhappy to see the tremendous eagerness with which they came to him, laying aside their brown bags. But what could he do? He could not run a charity show; that was impossible. He measured out their half-glass of coffee correct to the fraction of an inch, but they could cling to the glass as long as they liked.

The blind beggar, who whined for alms all day in front of 19 the big hotel, brought him part of his collection at the end of the day and demanded refreshment . . . and the grass-selling women. He disliked serving women; their shrill, loud voices got on his nerves. These came to him after disposing of headloads of grass satisfactorily. And that sly fellow with a limp who bought a packet of mixed fare every evening and carried it to a prostitute-like creature standing under a tree on the pavement opposite.

All the coppers that men and women of this part of the universe earned through their miscellaneous jobs ultimately came to him at the end of the day. He put all this money into a little cloth bag dangling from his neck under his shirt, and carried it home, soon after the night show had started at the theatre.

He lived in the second lane behind the market. His wife opened the door, throwing into the night air the scent of burnt oil which perpetually hung about their home. She snatched from his hands all his encumbrances, put her hand under his shirt to pull out his cloth bag and counted the cash immediately. They gloated over it. 'Five rupees invested in the morning has brought us another five . . .' They ruminated on the exquisite mystery of this multiplication. She put back into his cloth bag the capital for further investment on the morrow, and carefully separated the gains and put them away in a little wooden box that she had brought from her parents' house years before.

After dinner, he tucked a betel leaf and tobacco in his cheek and slept on the *pyol* of his house, and had dreams of traffic constables bullying him to move on and health inspectors saying that he was spreading all kinds of disease and depopulating the city. But fortunately in actual life no one bothered him very seriously. He gave an occasional packet of his stuff to the traffic constable going off duty or to the health-department menial who might pass that way.

The health officer no doubt came and said, 'You must put all this under a glass lid, otherwise I shall destroy it all some day . . . Take care!' But he was a kindly man who did not pursue any matter but wondered in private, 'How his customers survive his food, I can't understand! I suppose people build up a sort of immunity to such poisons, with all that dust blowing on it and the gutter behind . . .' Rama no doubt violated all the well-accepted canons of cleanliness and sanitation, but still his customers not only survived his fare but seemed actually to flourish on it, having consumed it for years without showing signs of being any the worse for it.

Rama's life could probably be considered a most satisfactory one, without agitation or heartburn of any kind. Why could it not go on forever, endlessly, till the universe itself cooled off and perished, when by any standard he could be proved to have led a life of pure effort? No one was hurt by his activity and money-making, and not many people could be said to have died of taking his stuff; there were no more casualties through his catering than, say, through the indifferent municipal administration.

But such security is unattainable in human existence. The gods grow jealous of too much contentment anywhere, and they show their displeasure all of a sudden. One night, when 21 he arrived as usual at his spot, he found a babbling crowd at the corner where he normally sat. He said authoritatively, 'Leave way, please.' But no one cared. It was the young shop-boy of the stationer's that plucked his sleeve and said, 'They have been fighting over something since the evening . . .'

'Over what?' asked Rama.

'Over something . . .' the boy said. 'People say someone was stabbed near the Sales Tax Office when he was distributing notices about some votes or something. It may be a private quarrel. But who cares? Let them fight who want a fight.'

Someone said, 'How dare you speak like that about us?'

Everyone turned to look at this man sourly. Someone in that crowd remarked, 'Can't a man speak . . .?'

His neighbour slapped him for it. Rama stood there with his load about him, looking on helplessly. This one slap was enough to set off a fuse. Another man hit another man, and then another hit another, and someone started a cry, 'Down with . . .'

'Ah, it is as we suspected, preplanned and organized to crush us,' another section cried.

People shouted, soda-water bottles were used as missiles. Everyone hit everyone else. A set of persons suddenly entered all the shops and demanded that these be closed. 'Why?' asked the shop-men.

'How can you have the heart to do business when . . .?'

The restraints of civilized existence were suddenly abandoned. Everyone seemed to be angry with everyone else.

Within an hour the whole scene looked like a battlefield. Of course the police came to the spot presently, but this made matters worse, since it provided another side to the fight. The police had a threefold task: of maintaining law and order and also maintaining themselves intact and protecting some party whom they believed to be injured. Shops that were not closed were looted.

The cinema house suddenly emptied itself of its crowd, which rushed out to enter the fray at various points. People with knives ran about, people with bloodstains groaned and shouted, ambulance vans moved here and there. The police used *lathis* and tear gas, and finally opened fire. Many people died. The public said that the casualties were three thousand, but the official communiqué maintained that only five were injured and four and a quarter killed in the police firing. At midnight Rama emerged from his hiding place under a culvert and went home.

The next day Rama told his wife, 'I won't take out the usual quantity. I doubt if there will be anyone there. God knows what devil has seized all those folk! They are ready to kill each other for some votes . . .' His instinct was right. There were more policemen than public on Market Road and his corner was strongly guarded. He had to set up his shop on a farther spot indicated by a police officer.

Matters returned to normal in about ten days, when all the papers clamoured for a full public inquiry into this or that: whether the firing was justified and what precautions were taken by the police to prevent this flare-up and so on. Rama watched the unfolding of contemporary history through the shouts of newsboys, and in due course tried to return to his corner. The moment he set up his tray and took his seat, a couple of young men wearing badges came to him and said, 'You can't have your shop here.'

'Why not, sir?'

'This is a holy spot on which our leader fell that day. The police aimed their guns at his heart. We are erecting a monument here. This is our place; the Municipality have handed this corner to us.'

Very soon this spot was cordoned off, with some congregation or the other always there. Money-boxes jingled for collections and people dropped coins. Rama knew better than anyone else how good the place was for attracting money. They collected enough to set up a memorial stone and, with an ornamental fencing and flower pots, entirely transformed the spot.

Austere, serious-looking persons arrived there and spoke among themselves. Rama had to move nearly two hundred yards away, far into the lane. It meant that he went out of the range of vision of his customers. He fell on their blind spot. The cinema crowd emerging from the theatre poured away from him; the *jutka*-drivers who generally left their vehicles on the roadside for a moment while the traffic constable showed indulgence and snatched a mouthful found it inconvenient to come so far; the boot-boys patronized a fellow on the opposite footpath, the scraggy pretender, whose fortunes seemed to be rising.

24    Nowadays Rama prepared a limited quantity of snacks for

sale, but even then he had to carry back remnants; he consumed some of it himself, and the rest, on his wife's advice, he warmed up and brought out for sale again next day. One or two who tasted the stuff reacted badly and spread the rumour that Rama's quality was not what it used to be. One night, when he went home with just two annas in his bag, he sat up on the *pyol* and announced to his wife, 'I believe our business is finished. Let us not think of it any more.'

He put away his pans and trays and his lamp, and prepared himself for a life of retirement. When all his savings were exhausted he went to one Restaurant Kohinoor, from which loudspeakers shrieked all day, and queued up for a job. For twenty rupees a month he waited eight hours a day on the tables. People came and went, the radio music frayed his nerves, but he stuck on; he had to. When some customer ordered him about too rudely, he said, 'Gently, brother. I was once a hotel-owner myself.' And with that piece of reminiscence he attained great satisfaction.

# Selvi

At the end of every concert, she was mobbed by autograph hunters. They would hem her in and not allow her to leave the dais. At that moment Mohan, slowly progressing towards the exit, would turn round and call across the hall, 'Selvi, hurry up. You want to miss the train?' 'Still a lot of time,' she could have said, but she was not in the habit of ever contradicting him; for Mohan this was a golden chance not to be missed, to order her in public and demonstrate his authority. He would then turn to a group of admirers waiting to escort him and Selvi, particularly Selvi, to the car, and remark in apparent jest, 'Left to herself, she'll sit there and fill all the autograph books in the world till doomsday, she has no sense of time.'

The public viewed her as a rare, ethereal entity; but he alone knew her private face. 'Not bad-looking,' he commented within himself when he first saw her, 'but needs touching up.' Her eyebrows, which flourished wildly, were trimmed and arched. For her complexion, by no means fair, but just on the borderline, he discovered the correct skin cream and talcum which imparted to her brow and cheeks a shade confounding classification. Mohan did not want anyone to suspect that he encouraged the use of cosmetics. He had been a follower of Mahatma Gandhi and spent several years in

prison, wore only cloth spun by hand and shunned all

luxury; there could be no question of his seeking modern, artificial aids to enhance the personality of his wife. But he had discovered at some stage certain subtle cosmetics through a contact in Singapore, an adoring fan of Selvi's, who felt only too honoured to be asked to supply them regularly, and to keep it a secret.

When Selvi came on the stage, she looked radiant, rather than dark, brown or fair, and it left the public guessing and debating, whenever the question came up, as to what colour her skin was. There was a tremendous amount of speculation on all aspects of her life and person wherever her admirers gathered, especially at a place like the Boardless where much town-talk was exchanged over coffee at the tables reserved for the habitués. Varma, the proprietor, loved to overhear such conversation from his pedestal at the cash counter, especially when the subject was Selvi. He was one of her worshippers, but from a distance, often feeling, 'Goddess Lakshmi has favoured me; I have nothing more to pray for in the line of wealth or prosperity, but I crave for the favour of the other goddess, that is Saraswathi, who is in our midst today as Selvi the divine singer; if only she will condescend to accept a cup of coffee or sweets from my hand, how grand it would be! But alas, whenever I bring a gift for her, *he* takes it and turns me back from the porch with a formal word of thanks.' Varma was only one among the thousands who had a longing to meet Selvi. But she was kept in a fortress of invisible walls. It was as if she was fated to spend her life either in solitary confinement or fettered to her gaoler in company. She was never left alone, even for a moment, with     27 anyone. She had been wedded to Mohan for over two decades and had never spoken to anyone except in his presence.

Visitors kept coming all day long for a *darshan* from Selvi, but few ever reached her presence. Some were received on the ground floor, some were received on the lawns, some were encouraged to go up the staircase – but none could get a glimpse of her, only of Mohan's secretary or of the secretary's secretary. Select personalities, however, were received ceremoniously in the main hall upstairs and seated on sofas. Ordinary visitors would not be offered seats, but they could occupy any bench or chair found scattered here and there and wait as long as they pleased – and go back wherever they came from.

Their home was a huge building of East India Company days, displaying arches, columns and gables, once the residence of Sir Frederick Lawley (whose statue stood in the town-square), who had kept a retinue of forty servants to sweep and dust the six oversized halls built on two floors, with tall doors and gothic windows and Venetian shutters, set on several acres of ground five miles away from the city on the road to Mempi Hills. The place was wooded with enormous trees; particularly important was an elm (or oak or beech, no one could say) at the gate, planted by Sir Frederick, who had brought the seedling from England, said to be the only one of its kind in India. No one would tenant the house, since Sir Frederick's spirit was said to hover about the place, and many weird tales were current in Malgudi at that time. The building had been abandoned since 1947, when Britain quit India. Mohan, who at some point made a bid for it, said, 'Let me try. Gandhiji's non-violence rid the country of the

British rule. I was a humble disciple of Mahatmaji and I should be able to rid the place of a British ghost by the same technique!' He found money to buy the house when Selvi received a fee for lending her voice to a film-star, who just moved her lips, synchronizing with Selvi's singing, and attained much glory for her performance in a film. But thereafter Mohan definitely shut out all film offers. 'I'll establish Selvi as a unique phenomenon on her own, not as a voice for some fat cosmetic-dummy.'

Bit by bit, by assiduous publicity and word-of-mouth recommendation, winning the favour of every journalist and music critic available, he had built up her image to its present stature. Hard work it was over the years. At the end, when it bore fruit, her name acquired a unique charm, her photograph began to appear in one publication or another every week. She was in demand everywhere. Mohan's office was besieged by the organizers of musical events from all over the country. 'Leave your proposal with my secretary, and we will inform you after finalizing our calendar for the quarter,' he would tell one. To another, he would say, 'My schedule is tight till 1982 – if there is any cancellation we'll see what can be done. Remind me in October of 1981, I'll give you a final answer.' He rejected several offers for no other reason than to preserve a rarity value for Selvi. When Mohan accepted an engagement, the applicant (more a supplicant) felt grateful, notwithstanding the exorbitant fee, of which half was to be paid immediately in cash without a receipt. He varied his tactics occasionally. He would specify that all the earnings of a certain concert should go to some 29 fashionable social-service organization carrying well-known names on its list of patrons. He would accept no remuneration for the performance itself, but ask for expenses in cash, which would approximate his normal fee. He was a financial expert who knew how to conjure up money and at the same time keep Income Tax at arm's length. Pacing his lawns and corridors restlessly, his mind was always busy, planning how to organize and manoeuvre men and money. Suddenly he would pause, summon his stenographer and dictate, or pick up the phone and talk at length into it.

In addition to the actual professional matters, he kept an eye on public relations, too; he attended select, exclusive parties, invited eminent men and women to dinner at Lawley Terrace; among the guests would often be found a sprinkling of international figures, too; on his walls hung group photographs of himself and Selvi in the company of the strangest assortment of personalities – Tito, Bulganin, Yehudi Menuhin, John Kennedy, the Nehru family, the Pope, Charlie Chaplin, yogis and sportsmen and political figures, taken under various circumstances and settings.

At the Boardless there was constant speculation about Selvi's early life. Varma heard at the gossip table that Selvi had been brought up by her mother in a back row of Vinayak Mudali Street, in a small house with tiles falling off, with not enough cash at home to put the tiles back on the roof, and had learnt music from her, practising with her brother and sister accompanying her on their instruments.

At this time Mohan had a photo studio on Market Road. Once Selvi's mother brought the girl to be photographed for a school magazine after she had won the first prize in a music competition. Thereafter Mohan visited them casually now and then, as a sort of well-wisher of the family, sat in the single chair their home provided, drank coffee and generally behaved as a benign god to that family by his advice and guidance. Sometimes he would request Selvi to sing, and then dramatically leave the chair and sit down on the floor crosslegged with his eyes shut, in an attitude of total absorption in her melody, to indicate that in the presence of such an inspired artist it would be blasphemous to sit high in a chair.

Day after day, he performed little services for the family, and then gradually took over the management of their affairs. At the Boardless, no one could relate with certainty at what point exactly he began to refer to Selvi as his wife or where, when or how they were married. No one would dare investigate it too closely now. Mohan had lost no time in investing the money earned from the film in buying Lawley Terrace. After freshening up its walls with lime wash and paints, on an auspicious day he engaged Gaffur's taxi, and took Selvi and the family to the Terrace.

While her mother, brother and sister grew excited at the dimension of the house as they passed through the six halls, looked up at the high ceilings and clicked their tongues, Selvi herself showed no reaction; she went through the house as if through the corridors of a museum. Mohan was a little disappointed and asked, 'How do you like this place?' At that all she could say in answer was, 'It looks big.' At the end of the guided tour, he launched on a description and history (avoiding the hauntings) of the house. She listened, without

31

any show of interest. Her mind seemed to be elsewhere.
They were all seated on the gigantic settees of the Company
days, which had come with the property, left behind because
they could not be moved. She didn't seem to notice even the
immensity of the furniture on which she was seated. As a
matter of fact, as he came to realize later, in the course of
their hundreds of concert tours she was habitually oblivious
of her surroundings. In any setting – mansion or Five Star
Hotel with luxurious guest rooms and attendants, or a small-
town or village home with no special facilities or privacy –
she looked equally indifferent or contented; washed, dressed
and was ready for the concert at the appointed time in the
evening. Most days she never knew or questioned where she
was to sing or what fee they were getting. Whenever he said,
'Pack and get ready,' she filled a trunk with her clothes,
toiletry and tonic pills, and was ready, not even questioning
where they were going. She sat in a reserved seat in the train
when she was asked to do so, and was ready to leave when
Mohan warned her they would have to get off at the next
stop. She was undemanding, uninquiring, uncomplaining.
She seemed to exist without noticing anything or anyone,
rapt in some secret melody or thought of her own.

In the course of a quarter-century, she had become a
national figure; travelled widely in and out of the country.
They named her the Goddess of Melody. When her name
was announced, the hall, any hall, filled up to capacity and
people fought for seats. When she appeared on the dais, the
audience was thrilled as if vouchsafed a vision, and she was
accorded a thundering ovation. When she settled down,

gently cleared her throat and hummed softly to help the accompanists tune their instruments, a silence fell among the audience. Her voice possessed a versatility and reach which never failed to transport her audience. Her appeal was alike to the common, unsophisticated listener as to pandits, theorists and musicologists, and even those who didn't care for any sort of music liked to be seen at her concerts for prestige's sake.

During a concert, wherever it might be – Madras, Delhi, London, New York or Singapore – Mohan occupied as a rule the centre seat in the first row of the auditorium and riveted his gaze on the singer, leaving people to wonder whether he was lost in her spell or whether he was inspiring her by thought-transference. Though his eyes were on her, his mind would be busy doing complicated arithmetic with reference to monetary problems, and he would also watch unobtrusively for any tape-recorder that might be smuggled into the hall (he never permitted recording), and note slyly the reactions of the VIPs flanking him.

He planned every concert in detail. He would sit up in the afternoon with Selvi and suggest gently but firmly, 'Wouldn't you like to start with the "Kalyani Varnam" – the minor one?' And she would say, 'Yes,' never having been able to utter any other word in her life. He would continue, 'The second item had better be Thiagaraja's composition in Begada, it'll be good to have a contrasting raga,' and then his list would go on to fill up about four hours. 'Don't bother to elaborate any *Pallavi* for this audience, but work out briefly a little detail in the Thodi composition. Afterwards you may 33 add any item you like, light *Bhajans*, *Javalis* or folk-songs,' offering her a freedom which was worthless since the programme as devised would be tight-fitting for the duration of the concert, which, according to his rule, should never exceed four hours. 'But for my planning and guidance, she'd make a mess, which none realizes,' he often reflected.

Everyone curried Mohan's favour and goodwill in the hope that it would lead him to the proximity of the star. Mohan did encourage a particular class to call on him and received them in the Central Hall of Lawley Terrace; he would call aloud to Selvi when such a person arrived, 'Here is So-and-so come.' It would be no ordinary name – only a minister or an inspector general of police or the managing director of a textile mill, or a newspaper editor, who in his turn would always be eager to do some favour for Mohan, hoping thereby to be recognized eventually by Selvi as a special friend of the family. Selvi would come out of her chamber ten minutes after being summoned and act her part with precision: a wonderful smile, and *namaste*, with her palms gently pressed together, which would send a thrill down the spine of the distinguished visitor, who would generally refer to her last concert and confess how deeply moving it had been, and how a particular raga kept ringing in his ears all that evening, long after the performance. Selvi had appropriate lines in reply to such praise: 'Of course, I feel honoured that my little effort has pleased a person of your calibre,' while Mohan would interpose with a joke or a personal remark. He didn't want any visitor, however important, to hold her attention, but would draw it to himself at the right moment. At the end Mohan would feel gratified that his tutored lines, gestures and expressions were perfectly delivered by Selvi. He would congratulate himself on shaping her so successfully into a celebrity. 'But for my effort, she'd still be another version of her mother and brother, typical Vinayak Mudali Street products, and nothing beyond that. I am glad I've been able to train her so well.'

In order that she might quickly get out of the contamination of Vinayak Mudali Street, he gently, unobtrusively, began to isolate her from her mother, brother and sister. As time went on, she saw less and less of them. At the beginning a car would be sent to fetch them, once a week; but as Selvi's public engagements increased, her mother and others were gradually allowed to fade out of her life. Selvi tried once or twice to speak to Mohan about her mother, but he looked annoyed and said, 'They must be all right. I'll arrange to get them – but where is the time for it? When we are able to spend at least three days at home, we will get them here.' Such a break was rare – generally they came home by train or car and left again within twenty-four hours. On occasions when they did have the time, and if she timidly mentioned her mother, he would almost snap, 'I know, I know, I'll send Mani to Vinayak Street – but some other time. We have asked the Governor to lunch tomorrow and they will expect you to sing, informally of course, for just thirty minutes.' 'The day after that?' Selvi would put in hesitantly, and he would ignore her and move off to make a telephone call. Selvi understood, and resigned herself to it, and never again mentioned her mother. 'If my own mother can't see me!' she 35 thought again and again, in secret anguish, having none to whom she could speak her feelings.

Mohan, noticing that she didn't bother him about her mother any more, felt happy that she had got over the obsession. 'That's the right way. Only a baby would bother about its mother.' He congratulated himself again on the way he was handling her.

Months and years passed thus. Selvi did not keep any reckoning of it, but went through her career like an automaton, switching on and off her music as ordered.

They were in Calcutta for a series of concerts when news of her mother's death reached her. When she heard it, she refused to come out of her room in the hotel, and wanted all her engagements cancelled. Mohan, who went into her room to coax her, swiftly withdrew when he noticed her tear-drenched face and dishevelled hair. All through the train journey back, she kept looking out of the window and never spoke a word, although Mohan did his best to engage her in talk. He was puzzled by her mood. Although she was generally not talkative, she would at least listen to whatever was said to her and intersperse an occasional monosyllabic comment. Now for a stretch of a thirty-six-hour journey she never spoke a word or looked in his direction. When they reached home, he immediately arranged to take her down to Vinayak Mudali Street, and accompanied her himself to honour the dead officially, feeling certain that his gesture would be appreciated by Selvi. Both the big car and Mohan in his whitest handspun clothes seemed ill-fitting in those surroundings. His car blocked half the street in which Selvi's mother had lived. Selvi's sister, who had married and had children in Singapore, could not come, and her brother's whereabouts were unknown . . . A neighbour dropped in to explain the circumstances of the old lady's death and how they had to take charge of the body and so forth. Mohan tried to cut short his narration and send him away, since it was unusual to let a nondescript talk to Selvi directly. But she said to Mohan, 'You may go back to the Terrace if you like. I'm staying here.' Mohan had not expected her to talk to him in that manner. He felt confused and muttered, 'By all means . . . I'll send back the car . . . When do you want it?'

'Never. I'm staying here as I did before . . .'

'How can you? In this street!' She ignored his objection and said, 'My mother was my guru; here she taught me music, lived and died . . . I'll also live and die here; what was good for her is good for me too . . .'

He had never known her to be so truculent or voluble. She had been for years so mild and complaisant that he never thought she could act or speak beyond what she was taught. He lingered, waited for a while hoping for a change of mood. Meanwhile, the neighbour was going on with his narration, omitting no detail of the old lady's last moments and the problems that arose in connection with the performance of the final obsequies. 'I did not know where to reach you, but finally we carried her across the river and I lit the pyre with my own hands and dissolved the ashes in the Sarayu. After all, I'd known her as a boy, and you remember how I used to call her Auntie and sit up and listen when you were practising . . . Oh! not these days of course, I can't afford to buy a ticket, or get anywhere near the hall where you sing.'

Mohan watched in consternation. He had never known her to go beyond the script written by him. She had never spoken to anyone or stayed in a company after receiving his signal to terminate the interview and withdraw. Today it didn't work. She ignored his signal, and the man from Vinayak neighbourhood went on in a frenzy of reliving the funeral; he felt triumphant to have been of help on a unique occasion.

After waiting impatiently, Mohan rose to go. 'Anything you want to be sent down?' 'Nothing,' she replied. He saw that she had worn an old sari, and had no makeup or jewellery, having left it all behind at the Terrace.

'You mean to say, you'll need nothing?'

'I need nothing . . .'

'How will you manage?' She didn't answer. He asked weakly, 'You have the series at Bhopal, shall I tell them to change the dates?' For the first time he was consulting her on such problems.

She simply said, 'Do what you like.'

'What do you mean by that?' No answer.

He stepped out and drove away; the car had attracted a crowd, which now turned its attention to Selvi. They came forward to stare at her – a rare luxury for most, the citadel having been impregnable all these years; she had been only a hearsay and a myth to most people. Someone said, 'Why did you not come to your mother's help? She was asking for you!' Selvi broke down and was convulsed with sobs.

Three days later Mohan came again to announce, 'On the thirtieth you have to receive an honorary degree at the Delhi

University . . .' She just shook her head negatively. 'The Prime Minister will be presiding over the function.'

When pressed, she just said, 'Please leave me out of all this, leave me alone, I want to be alone hereafter. I can't bear the sight of anyone . . .'

'Just this one engagement. Do what you like after that. Otherwise it will be most compromising. Only one day at Delhi, we will get back immediately – also you signed the gramophone contract for recording next month . . .' She didn't reply. Her look suggested that it was not her concern. 'You'll be landing me in trouble; at least, the present commitments . . .' It was difficult to carry on negotiations with a crowd watching and following every word of their talk. He wished he could have some privacy with her, but this was a one-room house, where everybody came and stood about or sat down anywhere. If he could get her alone, he would either coax her or wring her neck. He felt helpless and desperate, and suddenly turned round and left.

He came again a week later. But it proved no better. She neither welcomed him nor asked him to leave. He suggested to her to come to the car; this time he had brought his small car. She declined his invitation. 'After all, that woman was old enough to die,' he reflected. 'This fool is ruining her life . . .'

He allowed four more weeks for the mourning period and visited her again, but found a big gathering in her house, overflowing into the street. She sat at the back of the little hall, holding up her *thumbura*, and was singing to the audience as if it were an auditorium. A violinist and a drummer had 39 volunteered to play the accompaniments. 'She is frittering away her art,' he thought. She said, 'Come, sit down.' He sat in a corner, listened for a while and slipped away unobtrusively . . . Again and again, he visited her and found, at all hours of the day, people around her, waiting for her music. News about her free music sessions spread, people thronged there in cars, bicycles and on foot. Varma of the Boardless brought a box of sweets wrapped in gilt paper, and handed it to Selvi silently and went away, having realized his ambition to approach his goddess with an offering. Selvi never spoke unnecessarily. She remained brooding and withdrawn all day, not noticing or minding anyone coming in or going out.

Mohan thought he might be able to find her alone at least at night. At eleven o'clock one night he left his car in Market Road and walked to Vinayak Mudali Street. He called in softly through the door of Selvi's house, 'My dear, it's me, I have to talk to you urgently. Please open the door, please,' appealing desperately through the darkened house. Selvi opened a window shutter just a crack and said firmly, 'Go away, it's not proper to come here at this hour . . .' Mohan turned back with a lump in his throat, swearing half-aloud, 'Ungrateful wretch . . .'

# *Emden*

When he came to be named the oldest man in town, Rao's age was estimated anywhere between ninety and one hundred and five. He had, however, lost count of time long ago and abominated birthdays; especially after his eightieth, when his kinsmen from everywhere came down in a swarm and involved him in elaborate rituals, and with blaring pipes and drums made a public show of his attaining eighty. The religious part of it was so strenuous that he was laid up for fifteen days thereafter with fever. During the ceremony they poured pots of cold water, supposedly fetched from sacred rivers, over his head, and forced him to undergo a fast, while they themselves feasted gluttonously. He was so fatigued at the end of the day that he could hardly pose for the group photo, but flopped down in his chair, much to the annoyance of the photographer, who constantly withdrew his head from under the black hood to plead, 'Steady, please.' Finally, he threatened to pack up and leave unless they propped up the old gentleman. There were seventy-five heads to be counted in the group – all Rao's descendants one way or another. The photographer insisted upon splitting the group, as otherwise the individuals would be microscopic and indistinguishable on a single plate. That meant that after a little rest Rao had to be propped up a second time in the honoured seat. When he protested against this entire ceremony, they explained, 41

'It's a propitiatory ceremony to give you health and longevity.'

'Seems to me rather a device to pack off an old man quickly,' he said, at which his first daughter, herself past sixty, admonished him not to utter inauspicious remarks, when everyone was doing so much to help.

By the time he recovered from his birthday celebrations and the group photo in two parts could be hung on the wall, the house had become quiet and returned to its normal strength, which was about twenty in all – three of his sons and their families, an assortment of their children, nephews and nieces. He had his room in the right wing of the house, which he had designed and built in the last century as it looked. He had been the very first to buy a piece of land beyond Vinayak Street; it was considered an act of great daring in those days, being a deserted stretch of land from which thieves could easily slip away into the woods beyond, even in daylight; the place, however, developed into a residential colony and was named Ratnapuri, which meant City of Gems.

Rao's earlier years were spent in Kabir Street. When he came into his own and decided to live in style, he sold off their old house and moved to Ratnapuri. That was after his second wife had borne him four daughters, and the last of them was married off. He had moved along with his first wife's progeny, which numbered eight of varying ages. He seemed to be peculiarly ill-fated in matrimony – his uncle, who cast and read the stars for the whole family, used to say that Rao had Mars in the seventh house, with no other planet to checkmate its fury, and hence was bound to lose every wife. After the third marriage and more children, he was convinced of the malevolence of Mars. He didn't keep a record of the population at home – that was not his concern – his sons were capable of running the family and managing the crowd at home. He detached himself from all transactions and withdrew so completely that a couple of years past the grand ceremony of the eightieth birthday he could not remember the names of most of the children at home or who was who, or how many were living under his roof.

The eightieth birthday had proved a definite landmark in his domestic career. Aided by the dimming of his faculties, he could isolate himself with no effort whatever. He was philosophical enough to accept nature's readjustments: 'If I see less or hear less, so much the better. Nothing lost. My legs are still strong enough to take me about, and I can bathe and wash without help ... I enjoy my food and digest it.' Although they had a dining table, he refused to change his ancient habit of sitting on a rosewood plank on the floor and eating off a banana leaf in a corner of the dining hall. Everything for him went on automatically, and he didn't have to ask for anything, since his needs were anticipated; a daughter-in-law or niece or granddaughter or a great-grand someone or other was always there to attend him unasked. He did not comment or question, particularly not question, as he feared they would bawl in his left ear and strain their vocal cords, though if they approached his right ear he could guess what they might be saying. But he didn't care either way. His retirement was complete. He had worked hard all his life to establish himself, and provide for his family, each figure in the two-part group photograph owing its existence to him directly or indirectly. Some of the grandchildren had been his favourites at one time or another, but they had all grown out of recognition, and their names – oh, names! they were the greatest impediments to speech – every name remains on the tip of one's tongue but is gone when you want to utter it. This trick of nature reduces one to a state of babbling and stammering without ever completing a sentence. Even such a situation was acceptable, as it seemed to be ordained by nature to keep the mind uncluttered in old age.

He reflected and introspected with clarity in the afternoons – the best part of the day for him, when he had had his siesta; got up and had his large tumbler of coffee (brought to his room exactly at three by one of the ministering angels, and left on a little *teapoy* beside the door). After his coffee he felt revived, reclined in his easy-chair placed to catch the light at the northern window, and unfolded the morning paper, which, after everyone had read it, was brought and placed beside his afternoon coffee. Holding it close enough, he could read, if he wiped his glasses from time to time with a silk rag tied to the arm of his chair; thus comfortably settled, he half-read and half-ruminated. The words and acts of politicians or warmongers sounded stale – they spoke and acted in the same manner since the beginning of time; his eyes travelled down the columns – sometimes an advertisement caught his eye (nothing but an invitation to people to squander their money on all kinds of fanciful things), or

reports of deaths (not one recognizable name among the

dead). On the last page of the paper, however, half a column invariably gripped his attention – that was a daily report of a religious or philosophical discourse at some meeting at Madras; brief reports, but adequate for him to brush up his thoughts on God, on His incarnations and on definitions of Good and Evil. At this point, he would brood for a while and then fold and put away the paper exactly where he had found it, to be taken away later.

When he heard the hall clock chime four, he stirred himself to go out on a walk. This part of the day's routine was anticipated by him with a great thrill. He washed and put on a long shirt which came down to his knees, changed to a white dhoti, wrapped around his shoulder an embroidered cotton shawl, seized his staff and an umbrella and sallied out. When he crossed the hall, someone or other always cautioned him by bellowing, 'Be careful. Have you got the torch? Usual round? Come back soon.' He would just nod and pass on. Once outside, he moved with caution, taking each step only after divining the nature of the ground with the tip of his staff. His whole aim in life was to avoid a fall. One false step and that would be the end. Longevity was guaranteed as long as he maintained his equilibrium and verticality. This restriction forced him to move at snail's pace, and along a well-defined orbit every evening.

Leaving his gate, he kept himself to the extreme left of the street, along Vinayak Street, down Kabir Lane and into Market Road. He loved the bustle, traffic and crowds of Market Road – paused to gaze into shops and marvel at the crowd passing in and out perpetually. He shopped but rarely 45

– the last thing he remembered buying was a crayon set and a drawing book for some child at home. For himself he needed to buy only a particular brand of toothpowder (most of his teeth were still intact), for which he occasionally stopped at Chettiar's at the far end of Market Road, where it branched off to Ellaman Street. When he passed in front of the shop, the shopman would always greet him from his seat, 'How are you, sir? Want something to take home today?' Rao would shake his head and cross over to the other side of the road – this was the spot where his orbit curved back, and took him homeward, the whole expedition taking him about two hours. Before 6:30 he would be back at his gate, never having to use his torch, which he carried in his shirt pocket only as a precaution against any sudden eclipse of the sun or an unexpected nightfall.

The passage both ways would always be smooth and uneventful, although he would feel nervous while crossing the Market Gate, where Jayaraj the photo-framer always hailed him from his little shop, 'Grand Master, shall I help you across?' Rao would spurn that offer silently and pass on; one had to concentrate on one's steps to avoid bumping into the crowd at the Market Gate, and had no time for people like Jayaraj. After he had passed, Jayaraj, who enjoyed gossiping, would comment to his clients seated on a bench, 'At his age! Moves through the crowd as if he were in the prime of youth. Must be at least a hundred and ten! See his recklessness. It's not good to let him out like this. His people are indifferent. Not safe these days. With all these lorries, bicycles and auto-rickshaws, he'll come to grief someday, I'm sure . . .'

'Who's he?' someone might ask, perhaps a newcomer to the town, waiting for his picture to be framed.

'We used to call him Emden.* We were terrified of him when we were boys. He lived somewhere in Kabir Street. Huge, tall and imposing when he went down the road on his bicycle in his khaki uniform and a red turban and all kinds of badges. We took him to be a police inspector from his dress – not knowing that he wore the uniform of the Excise Department. He also behaved like the police – if he noticed anyone doing something he did not like, he'd go thundering at him, chase him down the street and lay the cane on his back. When we were boys, we used to loiter about the market in gangs, and if he saw us he'd scatter us and order us home. Once he caught us urinating against the school wall at Adam's Street, as we always did. He came down on us with a roar, seized four of us and shook us till our bones rattled, pushed us up before the headmaster and demanded, 'What are you doing, Headmaster? Is this the way you train them? Or do you want them to turn out to be guttersnipes? Why don't you keep an eye on them and provide a latrine in your school?' The headmaster rose in his seat, trembling and afraid to come too close to this terrible personality flourishing a cane. Oh, how many such things in his heyday! People were afraid of him. He might well have been a policeman for all his high-and-mighty style, but his business was only to check the taverns selling drinks – And you know how much he

*A German warship that shelled Madras in 1916, ever since, the term indicates anyone who is formidable and ruthless.

47

collected at the end of the day? Not less than five hundred rupees, that is, fifteen thousand a month, not even a governor could earn so much. No wonder he could build a fancy house at Ratnapuri and bring up his progeny in style. Oh, the airs that family give themselves! He narrowly escaped being prosecuted – if a national award were given for bribe-taking, it would go to him: when he was dismissed from service, he gave out that he had voluntarily retired! None the worse for it, has enough wealth to last ten generations. Emden! Indeed! He married several wives, seems to have worn them out one after another; that was in addition to countless sideshows, ha! ha! When we were boys, he was the talk of the town: some of us stealthily followed and spied on his movements in the dark lanes at night, and that provided us a lot of fun. He had great appetite for the unattached female tribe, such as nurses and schoolmistresses, and went after them like a bull! Emden, really! . . .' Jayaraj's tongue wagged while his hands were cutting, sawing and nailing a picture frame, and ceased the moment the work was finished, and he would end his narrations with: 'That'll be five rupees – special rate for you because you have brought the picture of Krishna, who is my family god. I've not charged for the extra rings for hanging . . .'

Rao kept his important papers stacked in an *almirah*, which he kept locked, and the key hidden under a lining paper in another cupboard where he kept his clothes and a few odds and ends, and the key of this second cupboard also was hidden somewhere, so that no one could have access to the two cupboards, which contained virtually all the clues to his life. Occasionally on an afternoon, at his hour of clarity and energy, he'd leave his easy-chair, bolt the door and open the first cupboard, take out the key under the paper lining, and then open the other cupboard containing his documents – title-deeds, diaries, papers and a will.

Today he finished reading the newspaper in ten minutes, and had reached his favourite column on the last page – the report of a discourse on reincarnations, to explain why one was born what he was and the working of the law of *karma*. Rao found it boring also: he was familiar with that kind of moralizing and philosophy. It was not four yet; the reading was over too soon. He found an unfilled half-hour between the newspaper reading and his usual time for the evening outing. He rose from the chair, neatly folded the newspaper and put it away on the little stool outside his door, and gently shut and bolted the door – noiselessly, because if they heard him shut the door, they would come up and caution him, 'Don't bolt,' out of fear that if he fell dead they might have to break the door open. Others were obsessed with the idea of *his* death as if they were all immortals!

He unlocked the cupboard and stood for a moment gazing at the papers tied into neat bundles – all the records of his official career from the start to his 'voluntary retirement' were there on the top shelf, in dusty and yellowing paper: he had shut the cupboard doors tight, yet somehow fine dust seeped in and settled on everything. He dared not touch anything for fear of soiling his fingers and catching a cold. He must get someone to destroy them, best to put them in a 49 fire; but whom could he trust? He hated the idea of anyone reading those memos from the government in the latter days of his service – he'd prefer people not to know the official mess and those threats of inquiries before he quit the service. The Secretary to the Government was a demon out to get his blood – inspired by anonymous letters and backbiters. Only one man had stood by him – his first assistant, wished he could remember his name or whereabouts – good fellow; if he were available he'd set him to clean and arrange his *almirah* and burn the papers: he'd be dependable, and would produce the ash if asked. But who was he? He patted his forehead as if to jerk the memory-machine into action . . . And then his eyes roved down to the next shelf; he ran his fingers over them lovingly – all documents relating to his property and their disposal after his death. No one in the house could have any idea of it or dare come near them. He must get the lawyer-man (what was his name again?) and closet himself with him someday. He was probably also dead. Not a soul seemed to be left in town . . . Anyway, must try to send someone to fetch him if he was alive, it was to be done secretly. How? Somehow.

His eyes travelled to a shelf with an assortment of packets containing receipts, bills and several diaries. He had kept a diary regularly for several years, recording a bit of daily observation or event on each page. He always bought the same brand of diary, called 'Matchless' – of convenient size, ruled pages, with a flap that could be buttoned so that no one could casually open its pages and read its contents. The
Matchless Stationery Mart off the main market manufactured

it. On the last day of every December he would stop by for a copy costing four rupees — rather expensive but worth the price . . . more often than not the man would not take money for it, as he'd seek some official favour worth much more. Rao was not the sort to mind dispensing his official favours if it helped some poor soul. There was a stack of thirty old diaries in there (at some point in his life, he had abandoned the practice), which contained the gist of all his day-to-day life and thought: that again was something, an offering for the God of Fire before his death. He stood ruminating at the sight of the diaries. He pulled out one from the stack at random, wiped the thin layer of dust with a towel, went back to his chair and turned over the leaves casually. The diary was fifty-one years old. After glancing through some pages, he found it difficult to read his own close calligraphy in black ink and decided to put it back, as it was time to prepare for his walk. However, he said to himself, 'Just a minute. Let me see what I did on this date, on the same day, so long ago . . .' He looked at the calendar on the wall. The date was the twentieth of March. He opened the diary and leafed through the earlier pages, marvelling at the picture they presented of his early life: what a lot of activities morning till night, connected with the family, office and personal pursuits! His eyes smarted; he skipped longer passages and concentrated on the briefer ones. On the same day fifty-one years ago — the page contained only four lines, which read: 'Too lenient with S. She deserves to be taught a lesson . . .' This triggered a memory, and he could almost hear the echo of his own shouting at somebody, and the next few lines indicated the course of action: 'Thrashed her soundly for her own good and left. Will not see her again . . . How can I accept the responsibility? She must have had an affair – after all a DG.*. Wish I had locked her in before leaving.' He studied this entry dispassionately. He wondered who it was. The initial was not helpful. He had known no one with a name beginning with S. Among the ladies he had favoured in his days, it could be anyone . . . but names were elusive anyway.

With great effort, he kept concentrating on this problem. His forehead throbbed with the strain of concentration. Of course, the name eluded him, but the geography was coming back to him in fragments. From Chettiar Stores . . . yes, he remembered going up Market Road . . . and noted the light burning at the shop facing him even at a late hour when returning home; that meant he had gone in that narrow street branching off from Market Road at that point, and that led to a parallel street . . . from there one went on and on and twisted and turned in a maze of by-lanes and reached that house – a few steps up before tapping gently on the rosewood door studded with brass stars, which would open at once as if she was waiting on the other side; he'd slip in and shut the door immediately, lest the neighbours be watching, and retrace his steps at midnight. But he went there only two days in the week, when he had free time . . . Her name, no, could not get it, but he could recollect her outline rather hazily – fair, plump and loving and jasmine-smelling; he was definite that the note referred to this woman, and not to

*Dancing Girl, a term denoting a public woman in those days.

another one, also plump and jasmine-smelling somewhere not so far away . . . he remembered slapping a face and flouncing out in a rage. The young fellow was impetuous and hot-blooded . . . must have been someone else, not himself in any sense. He could not remember the house, but there used to be a coconut palm and a well in the street in front of the house . . . it suddenly flashed across his mind that the name of the street was Gokulam.

He rose and locked away the diary and secreted the key as usual, washed and dressed, and picked up his staff and umbrella and put on his sandals, with a quiet thrill. He had decided to venture beyond his orbit today, to go up and look for the ancient rosewood, brass-knobbed door, beside the coconut tree in that maze. From Chettiar Stores, his steps were bound to lead him on in the right direction, and if S. was there and happened to stand at the street door, he'd greet her . . . he might not be able to climb the four steps, but he'd offer her a small gift and greeting from the street. She could come down and take it. He should not have slapped her face . . . he had been impetuous and cruel. He should not have acted on jealousy . . . he was filled with remorse. After all, she must have shown him a great deal of kindness and given him pleasure ungrudgingly – otherwise, why would one stay until midnight?

While he tap-tapped his way out of his house now, someone in the hall inquired as usual, 'Got your torch? Rather late today. Take care of yourself.' He was excited. The shopman on the way, who habitually watched and commented, noted that the old man was moving rather jauntily today. 'Oh,  53

Respected One, good day to you, sir,' said Mani from his cycle shop. 'In such a hurry today? Walk slowly, sir, road is dug up everywhere.' Rao looked up and permitted himself a gentle nod of recognition. He did not hear the message, but he could guess what Mani might be saying. He was fond of him – a great-grandson of that fellow who had studied with him at Albert Mission School. Name? As usual Mani's great-grandfather's name kept slipping away . . . he was some Ram or Shankar or something like that. Oh, what a teaser! He gave up and passed on. He kept himself to the edge as usual, slowed down his pace after Mani's advice; after all, his movement should not be noticeable, and it was not good to push oneself in that manner and pant with the effort.

At Jagan's Sweets, he halted. Some unknown fellow at the street counter. Children were crowding in front of the stall holding forth money and asking for this and that. They were blocking the way. He waited impatiently and tapped his staff noisily on the ground till the man at the counter looked up and asked, 'Anything, master?' Rao waved away the children with a flourish of his stick and approached the counter and feasted his eyes on the heaped-up sweets in different colours and shapes, and wished for a moment he could eat recklessly as he used to. But perhaps that'd cost him his life today – the secret of his survival being the spartan life he led, rigorously suppressing the cravings of the palate. He asked, 'What's fresh today?' The man at the counter said, 'We prepare everything fresh every day. Nothing is yesterday's . . .' Rao could only partly guess what he was saying but, without betraying himself, said, 'Pack up *jilebi* for three rupees . . .'

He counted out the cash carefully, received the packet of *jilebi*, held it near his nostrils (the smell of food would not hurt, and there was no medical advice against it), for a moment relishing its rose-scented flavour; and was on his way again. Arriving at the point of Chettiar Stores, he paused and looked up at his right – yes, that street was still there as he had known it . . .

Noticing him hesitating there, the shop man hailed from his shop, 'Oh, Grand Master, you want anything?' He felt annoyed. Why couldn't they leave him alone? And then a young shop assistant came out to take his order. Rao looked down at him and asked, pointing at the cross street, 'Where does it lead?'

'To the next street,' the boy said, and that somehow satisfied him. The boy asked, 'What can I get you?'

'Oh, will no one leave me alone?' Rao thought with irritation. They seemed to assume that he needed something all the time. He hugged the packet of sweets close to his chest, along with the umbrella slung on the crook of his arm. The boy seemed to be bent on selling him something. And so he said, 'Have you sandalwood soap?' He remembered that S., or whoever it was, used to be fond of it. The boy got it for him with alacrity. Its fragrance brought back some old memories. He had thought there was a scent of jasmine about S., but he realized now that it must have been that of sandalwood. He smelt it nostalgically before thrusting it into his pocket. 'Anything else, sir?' asked the boy. 'No, you may go,' and he crossed Market Road over to the other side.

Trusting his instinct to guide him, he proceeded along the 55 cross street ahead of Chettiar Stores. It led to another street running parallel, where he took a turn to his left on an impulse, and then again to his right into a lane, and then left, and then about-turn – but there was no trace of Gokulam Street. As he tap-tapped along, he noticed a cobbler on the roadside, cleared his throat, struck his staff on the ground to attract attention and asked, 'Here, which way to Gokulam Street?' At first, the cobbler shook his head, then, to get rid of the inquirer, pointed vaguely in some direction and resumed his stitching. 'Is there a coconut tree in this street?' The other once again pointed along the road. Rao felt indignant. 'Haughty beggar,' he muttered. 'In those days I'd have . . .' He moved on, hoping he'd come across the landmark. He stopped a couple of others to ask the same question, and that did not help. No coconut tree anywhere. He was sure that it was somewhere here that he used to come, but everything was changed. All the generations of men and women who could have known Gokulam Street and the coconut tree were dead – new generations around here, totally oblivious of the past. He was a lone survivor.

He moved cautiously now, as the sun was going down. He became rather nervous and jabbed his staff down at each step, afraid of stumbling into a hole. It was a strain moving in this fashion, so slow and careful, and he began to despair that he'd ever reach the Market Road again. He began to feel anxious, regretted this expedition. The family would blame him if he should have a mishap. Somehow he felt more disturbed at the thought of their resentment than of his own possible suffering. But he kept hobbling along steadily. Some passers-by paused to stare at him and comment on his perambulation. At some point, his staff seemed to stab through a soft surface; at the same moment a brown mongrel, which had lain curled up in dust, in perfect camouflage, sprang up with a piercing howl; Rao instinctively jumped, as he had not done for decades, luckily without falling down, but the packet of *jilebi* flew from his grip and landed in front of the mongrel, who picked it up and trotted away, wagging his tail in gratitude. Rao looked after the dog helplessly and resumed his journey homeward. Brooding over it, he commented to himself, 'Who knows, S. is perhaps in this incarnation now . . .'

# House Opposite

The hermit invariably shuddered when he looked out of his window. The house across the street was occupied by a shameless woman. Late in the evening, men kept coming and knocking on her door – afternoons, too, if there was a festival or holiday. Sometimes they lounged on the *pyol* of her house, smoking, chewing tobacco, and spitting into the gutter – committing all the sins of the world, according to the hermit who was striving to pursue a life of austerity, forswearing family, possessions, and all the comforts of life. He found this single-room tenement with a couple of coconut trees and a well at the backyard adequate, and the narrow street swarmed with children: sometimes he called in the children, seated them around, and taught them simple moral lessons and sacred verse. On the walls he had nailed a few pictures of gods cut out of old calendars, and made the children prostrate themselves in front of them before sending them away with a piece of sugar candy each.

His daily life followed an unvarying pattern. Bird-like, he retired at dusk, lying on the bare floor with a wooden block under his head for a pillow. He woke up at four ahead of the rooster at the street corner, bathed at the well, and sat down on a piece of deerskin to meditate. Later he lit the charcoal stove and baked a few *chapattis* for breakfast and lunch and cooked certain restricted vegetables and greens, avoiding potato, onion, okra, and such as might stimulate the baser impulses.

Even in the deepest state of meditation, he could not help hearing the creaking of the door across the street when a client left after a night of debauchery. He rigorously suppressed all cravings of the palate, and punished his body in a dozen ways. If you asked him why, he would have been at a loss to explain. He was the antithesis of the athlete who flexed his muscles and watched his expanding chest before a mirror. Our hermit, on the contrary, kept a minute check of his emaciation and felt a peculiar thrill out of such an achievement. He was only following without questioning his ancient guru's instructions, and hoped thus to attain spiritual liberation.

One afternoon, opening the window to sweep the dust on the sill, he noticed her standing on her doorstep, watching the street. His temples throbbed with the rush of blood. He studied her person – chiselled features, but sunk in fatty folds. She possessed, however, a seductive outline; her forearms were cushion-like and perhaps the feel of those encircling arms attracted men. His gaze, once it had begun to hover about her body, would not return to its anchor – which should normally be the tip of one's nose, as enjoined by his guru and the yoga *shastras*.

Her hips were large, thighs stout like banana stalks, on the whole a mattress-like creature on which a patron could loll all night without a scrap of covering – 'Awful monster! Personification of evil.' He felt suddenly angry. Why on earth should that creature stand there and ruin his tapas: all the merit he 59 had so laboriously acquired was draining away like water through a sieve. Difficult to say whether it was those monstrous arms and breasts or thighs which tempted and ruined men . . . He hissed under his breath, 'Get in, you devil, don't stand there!' She abruptly turned round and went in, shutting the door behind her. He felt triumphant, although his command and her compliance were coincidental. He bolted the window tight and retreated to the farthest corner of the room, settled down on the deerskin, and kept repeating, 'Om, Om, Rama, Jayarama': the sound 'Rama' had a potency all its own – and was reputed to check wandering thoughts and distractions. He had a profound knowledge of mantras and their efficacy. 'Sri Rama . . .' he repeated, but it was like a dilute and weak medicine for high fever. It didn't work. 'Sri Rama, Jayarama . . .' he repeated with a desperate fervour, but the effect lasted not even a second. Unnoticed, his thoughts strayed, questioning: who was that fellow in a check shirt and silk upper cloth over his shoulder descending the steps last evening when I went out to the market? Seen him somewhere . . . where? when? . . . ah, he was the big tailor on Market Road . . . with fashionable men and women clustering round him! Master-cutter who was a member of two or three clubs . . . Hobnobbed with officers and businessmen – and this was how he spent his evening, lounging on the human mattress! And yet fashionable persons allowed him to touch them with his measuring tape! Contamination, nothing but contamination; sinful life. He cried out in the lonely room, 'Rama! Rama!' as if hailing someone hard of hearing. Presently he realized it was a futile exercise. Rama was a perfect incarnation, of course, but he was mild and gentle until provoked beyond limit, when he would storm and annihilate the evildoer without a trace, even if he was a monster like Ravana. Normally, however, he had forbearance, hence the repetition of his name only resulted in calmness and peace, but the present occasion demanded stern measures. God Siva's mantra should help. Did he not open his Third Eye and reduce the God of Love to ashes, when the latter slyly aimed his arrow at him while he was meditating? Our hermit pictured the god of matted locks and fiery eyes and recited aloud: 'Om Namasivaya,' that lonely hall resounding with his hoarse voice. His rambling, unwholesome thoughts were halted for a while, but presently regained their vigour and raced after the woman. She opened her door at least six times on an evening. Did she sleep with them all together at the same time? He paused to laugh at this notion, and also realized that his meditation on the austere god was gone. He banged his fist on his temples, which pained but improved his concentration. 'Om Namasivaya . . .' Part of his mind noted the creaking of the door of the opposite house. She was a serpent in whose coils everyone was caught and destroyed – old and young and the middle-aged, tailors and students (he had noticed a couple of days ago a young B.Sc. student from Albert Mission Hostel at her door), lawyers and magistrates (Why not?) . . . No wonder the world was getting overpopulated – with such pressure of the elemental urge within every individual! O God Siva, this woman must be eliminated. He would confront her some day and tell her to get out. He would tell her, 'Oh, sinful wretch, who is spreading disease 61 and filth like an open sewer: think of the contamination you have spread around – from middle-aged tailor to B.Sc. student. You are out to destroy mankind. Repent your sins, shave your head, cover your ample loins with sackcloth, sit at the temple gate and beg or drown yourself in *sarayu* after praying for a cleaner life at least in the next birth . . .'

Thus went his dialogue, the thought of the woman never leaving his mind, during all the wretched, ill-spent night; he lay tossing on the bare floor. He rose before dawn, his mind made up. He would clear out immediately, cross Nallappa's Grove, and reach the other side of the river. He did not need a permanent roof; he would drift and rest in any temple or *mantap* or in the shade of a banyan tree: he recollected an ancient tale he had heard from his guru long ago . . . A harlot was sent to heaven when she died, while her detractor, a self-righteous reformer, found himself in hell. It was explained that while the harlot sinned only with her body, her detractor was corrupt mentally, as he was obsessed with the harlot and her activities, and could meditate on nothing else.

Our hermit packed his wicker box with his sparse possessions – a god's image in copper, a rosary, the deerskin, and a little brass bowl. Carrying his box in one hand, he stepped out of the house, closing the door gently behind him. In the dim hour of the dusk, shadowy figures were moving – a milkman driving his cow ahead, labourers bearing crowbars and spades, women with baskets on their way to the market. While he paused to take a final look at the shelter he was abandoning, he heard a plaintive cry, 'Swamiji' from the opposite house, and saw the woman approach him with a tray, heaped with fruits and flowers. She placed it at his feet and said in a low reverential whisper: 'Please accept my offering. This is a day of remembrance of my mother. On this day I pray and seek a saint's blessing. Forgive me . . .' All the lines he had rehearsed for a confrontation deserted him at this moment; looking at her flabby figure, the dark rings under her eyes, he felt pity. As she bent down to prostrate, he noticed that her hair was indifferently dyed and that the parting in the middle widened into a bald patch over which a string of jasmine dangled loosely. He touched her tray with the tip of his finger as a token of acceptance, and went down the street without a word.

# The Watchman

There was still a faint splash of red on the western horizon. The watchman stood on the tank bund and took a final survey. All the people who had come for evening walks had returned to their homes. Not a soul anywhere – except that obstinate angler, at the northern end, who sat with his feet in water, sadly gazing on his rod. It was no use bothering about him: he would sit there till midnight, hoping for a catch.

The Taluk office gong struck nine. The watchman was satisfied that no trespassing cattle had sneaked in through the wire fencing. As he turned to go, he saw, about a hundred yards away, a shadowy figure moving down the narrow stone steps that led to the water's edge. He thought for a second that it might be a ghost. He dismissed the idea, and went up to investigate. If it was anyone come to bathe at this hour . . . From the top step he observed that it was a woman's form. She stooped over the last step and placed something on it – possibly a letter. She then stepped into knee-deep water, and stood there, her hands pressed together in prayer. Unmistakable signs – always to be followed by the police and gruesome details, bringing the very worst possible reputation to a tank.

He shouted, 'Come out, there, come out of it.' The form looked up from the water. 'Don't stand there and gaze. You'll catch a cold, come up whoever you are . . .' He raced down the steps and picked up the letter. He hurriedly lit his lamp, and turned its wick till it burnt brightly, and held it up, murmuring: 'I don't like this. Why is everyone coming to the same tank? If you want to be dead, throw yourself under an engine,' he said.

The light fell upon the other's face. It was a young girl's, wet with tears. He felt a sudden pity. He said, 'Sit down, sit down and rest ... no, no ... go up two more steps and sit down. Don't sit so near the water ...' She obeyed. He sat down on the last step between her and the water, placed the lantern on the step, took out a piece of tobacco, and put it in his mouth. She buried her face in her hands, and began to sob. He felt troubled and asked: 'Why don't you rise and go home, lady?'

She sputtered through her sob: 'I have no home in this world!'

'Don't tell me! Surely, you didn't grow up without a home all these years!' said the watchman.

'I lost my mother when I was five years old –' she said.

'I thought so ...' replied the watchman, and added, 'and your father married again and you grew up under the care of your stepmother?'

'Yes, yes, how do you know?' she asked.

'I am sixty-five years old,' he said and asked, 'Did your stepmother trouble you?'

'No, there you are wrong,' the girl said. 'She is very kind to me. She has been looking after me ever since my father died a few years ago. She has just a little money on hand left by my father, and she spends it on us.'

The watchman looked at the stars, sighed for the dinner that he was missing. 'It's very late, madam, go home.'

'I tell you I've no home –' she retorted angrily.

'Your stepmother's house is all right from what you say. She is good to you.'

'But why should I be a burden to her? Who am I?'

'You are her husband's daughter,' the watchman said, and added, 'That is enough claim.'

'No, no. I won't live on anybody's charity.'

'Then you will have to wait till they find you a husband –'

She glared at him in the dark. 'That's what I do not want to do. I want to study and become a doctor and earn my livelihood. I don't want to marry. I often catch my mother talking far into the night to her eldest son, worrying about my future, about my marriage. I know they cannot afford to keep me in college very long now; it costs about twenty rupees a month.'

'Twenty rupees!' the watchman exclaimed. It was his month's salary. 'How can anybody spend so much for books!'

'Till today,' she said, 'I was hoping that I would get a scholarship. That would have saved me. But this evening they announced; others have got it, not I. My name is not there –' and she broke down again. The watchman looked at her in surprise. He comprehended very little of all this situation. She added: 'And when they come to know of this, they will try to arrange my marriage. Someone is coming to have a look at me tomorrow.'

'Marry him and may God bless you with ten children.'

'No, no,' she cried hysterically. 'I don't want to marry. I want to study.'

The silent night was stabbed by her sobbing and some

night bird rustled the water, and wavelets beat upon the shore. Seeing her suffer, he found his own sorrows in life came to his mind; how in those far-off times, in his little village home an epidemic of cholera laid out his father and mother and brothers on the same day, and he was the sole survivor; how he was turned out of his ancestral home through the trickery of his father's kinsmen, and he wandered as an orphan, suffering indescribable hunger and privation.

'Everyone has his own miseries,' he said. 'If people tried to kill themselves for each one of them, I don't know how often they would have to drown.' He remembered further incidents and his voice shook with sorrow. 'You are young and you don't know what sorrow is . . .' He remained silent and a sob broke out of him as he said: 'I prayed to all the gods in the world for a son. My wife bore me eight children. Only one daughter lives now, and none of the others saw the eleventh year . . .' The girl looked at him in bewilderment.

The Taluk office gong struck again. 'It is late, you had better get up and go home,' he said.

She replied: 'I have no home.'

He felt irritated. 'You are making too much of nothing. You should not be obstinate –'

'You don't know my trouble,' she said.

He picked up his lantern and staff and got up. He put her letter down where he found it.

'If you are going to be so obstinate, I'll leave you alone. No one can blame me.' He paused for a moment, looked at her, and went up the steps, not a word passed between them again.

The moment he came back to duty next morning, he hurried down the stone steps. The letter lay where he had dropped it on the previous night. He picked it up and gazed on it, helplessly, wishing that it could tell him about the fate of the girl after he had left her. He tore it up and flung it on the water. As he watched the bits float off on ripples, he blamed himself for leaving her and going away on the previous night. 'I am responsible for at least one suicide in this tank,' he often remarked to himself. He could never look at the blue expanse of water again with an easy mind. Even many months later he could not be certain that the remains of a body would not come up all of a sudden. 'Who knows, it sometimes happens that the body gets stuck deep down,' he reflected.

Years later, one evening as he stood on the bund and took a final survey before going home, he saw a car draw up on the road below. A man, a woman, and three children emerged from the car and climbed the bund. When they approached, the watchman felt a start at his heart; the figure and face of the woman seemed familiar to him. Though the woman was altered by years, and ornaments, and dress, he thought that he had now recognized the face he had once seen by the lantern light. He felt excited at this discovery. He had numerous questions to ask. He brought together his palms and saluted her respectfully. He expected she would stop and speak to him. But she merely threw at him an indifferent glance and passed on. He stood staring after her for a moment, baffled. 'Probably this is someone else,' he muttered and turned to go home, resolving to dismiss the whole episode from his mind.

68

# A Career

The Talkative Man said:

Years and years ago I had a shop. It was in those days
when Lawley Extension was not what it is now. It consisted
of fewer than a hundred houses. Market Road being at least a
mile off, the people living in the Extension looked on me as a
saviour when I took up a little building, and on an auspicious
day hung up a large board with the inscription: THE NA-
TIONAL PROVISION STORES. I went from house to house and
secured orders. I literally examined every pantry in the
Extension and filled up the gaps. When the bell rang for the
midday interval at the Extension Elementary School, children
swarmed into my shop and carried off whatever sweets,
ribbons, and fancy stationery I happened to keep. I did about
twenty-five rupees credit and ten rupees cash sales every day.
This gave us at least fifty rupees a month to live on. We paid
a rent of five rupees and took a small house in Kabir Street,
which was over a mile from my shop. I left at seven in the
morning and returned home only at nine in the evening, after
clearing the daily accounts.

A year and a half passed thus. One day a young fellow
presented himself at my shop. He looked about twenty, very
fair and bright. He wore a spotless dhoti and shirt.

'What can I do for you?' I asked, taking him to be a young
customer.

In answer he brought his palms together in salute and said, 'I need your help, sir. I will do whatever work you may give me in return for a little food and shelter and kindness.'

There was something in the young fellow's personality which appealed to me. Moreover, he had on his forehead three-finger width of sacred ash and a dot of vermilion between his eyebrows. He looked as if he had just come from a temple.

'I am very God-fearing, sir, and susceptible to religious influences.'

I spoke to him for about an hour.

He said he belonged to a family of wealthy landholders in a village near Trichinopoly. His mother had died some years before. His father took a mistress who ill-treated the boy and consequently he ran away from home.

A touching story, I felt.

I directed him to my house. When I went home in the evening I found that he had already made himself a great favourite there. His life story had deeply moved my wife.

'So young!' she whispered to me, 'And to think that he should be left at this age without a father or a mother!' she sighed. He had made himself lovable in a dozen ways already. He had taken my little son out for a walk. The youngster cried as soon as he came home, 'Let Ramu stay in our house. He is great. He knows magic and can tame tigers and elephants.' Ramu walked into the kitchen and offered assistance. At first my wife protested.

'Why won't you allow me to go near the oven, Mother?' he asked. 'Is it because you think I can't cook? Give me a chance and see.'

He made a dash for the bathroom, turned the tap on himself, and came out dripping. He took a handful of sacred ash and smeared it on his forehead. My wife was tremendously impressed. She let him do the cooking.

He prepared delicious food for us. We were all very pleased. After that he helped my wife with all the cleaning and scrubbing. He slept at night on the bare floor, refusing the mat and the pillow we offered.

He was the first to be up next morning. He lit the stove and woke up my wife. At midday he brought me my food. While I ate he attended to the school children who came into the shop. He handed them their knick-knacks with an expert hand. He charmed and amused them. He made them laugh. He beguiled them with an alternative when he had not on hand what they wanted.

It was inevitable that in a month he should be sharing with me the shop work. He had attractive ways about him. Customers liked to talk to him. Within a short time there was not a single home in the Extension where he was not treated as a member of the family. He knew the inside story of every family. He served everyone to the best of his capacity. Here he helped a man with his garden, and there he pleaded with a house-building contractor and had an estimate revised. He patched up quarrels. He tamed truants and sent them to school. He took part in all the extracurricular activities of the Extension Elementary School. He took an interest in the Club Movement. He dressed himself up for the occasion when the inspector visited the school, and arranged for the supply of garlands and flowers. And all this in addition to assisting me in the shop. He went every day to the market and purchased provisions from the wholesale merchants, sat down for hours on end in the shop and handed out things to customers, pored over the accounts till late at night, and collected all the bills.

As a result of Ramu's presence my business increased nearly tenfold. I had abundant rest now. I left the shop entirely in his hands. I went home for food at midday. After that I slept till three in the afternoon. And then I went to the shop, but stayed there only till five o'clock, when I went to an open space nearby and played badminton with some friends. I came to the shop again only at seven in the evening.

Once or twice my wife and I talked over the matter and tried to fix up a monthly pay for Ramu. We felt we ought not to be exploiting Ramu's friendliness. But when the subject was mentioned Ramu grew red in the face and said, 'If you don't want me to stay with you any more, you may talk of salary again . . .'

Five years passed thus. He aged with us. He lived with us through all our joys and sorrows. I had four children now. My business had prospered enormously. We were living in a bigger house in the same street. I took the shop building on a long lease. I had an immense stock of all kinds of provisions and goods.

I extended my business. I purchased large quantities of butter in all the nearby villages and sold them to butter and ghee merchants in Madras. This business gave me large profits. It kept me running between the villages and Madras. The shop was entirely in Ramu's hands.

At Madras I used to stop with a merchant in George Town. Once work kept me on there a little longer than I had anticipated. One evening just as I was starting out to post a letter for Ramu, a telegraph messenger stepped off his cycle and gave me an envelope. I tore open the cover and read: 'Father dying of cholera. Must go at once. Return immediately. Ramu.'

The next morning at five o'clock I got down at Malgudi. Ramu was at the station. He was going to Trichinopoly by the same train. The train halted only for a few minutes. Red-eyed and sobbing, Ramu said, 'My father, father, cholera. Never thought he would get it . . .' I consoled him. I had never seen him so broken. I said feebly, 'He will be all right, don't worry . . .' I had hardly the heart to ask him about the shop. He himself said, 'I have handed the keys to Mother, and all the accounts and cash also . . .'

'All right, all right, I will look to all that. Don't worry,' I said.

The guard blew his whistle. Ramu jumped into a third-class compartment. The train jerked forward. He put his head out the window and said, 'I will be back tomorrow by the night train, if my father gets better . . . Whatever happens, I won't be away for more than fifteen days. Kittu has asked me to bring him' – his voice and face receded – 'a wooden elephant on wheels. Please tell him that I will surely bring it. My *namaskarams* to Mother . . .' Tears rolled down his cheeks. Even long after the train had left the platform he was still looking out of the window and gesticulating to indicate 'I will surely be back soon . . .'

Having some unfinished Madras business on hand, I could hardly go near the shop for a week. When I reopened, the first thing that I noticed was that the shop was empty. Except for a bag of coarse rice and a few bars of cheap soap, all the racks and containers were empty. I picked up the books and examined them. The entries were all in a mess. I put them away. Replenishing the stock was more urgent. I made out a list and went to the market.

Sadik Sait, my wholesale supplier, squatted amidst his cushions and welcomed me warmly. I owed my start in life to the unlimited credit he allowed me. After some preliminary, inconsequential talk, I put before him the list. He scrutinized it gloomily and shook his head. He said, 'You want goods for about three hundred rupees. I wouldn't advise you to put up your dues. Why don't you take fifty rupees' worth now? I am suggesting this only for your own convenience . . .' This was the first time in my life that he had spoken to me in this manner. And he explained, 'Don't mistake me, friend. You are a business man, so am I. No use talking indirectly and vaguely. I will tell you what the matter is. Your account with us stands at Rs. 3,500 – and if you had paid at least a single instalment for these three months, we should have felt happier . . .'

'But, Sait, last month I sent four hundred to be given to you, and the month before three hundred and fifty, and the month before – There must be only a balance of –' He took out his ledger. There was only one payment made for four months when the bill stood at about a thousand. After that there had been purchases almost every day for about forty rupees.

'The young fellow said that business was very brisk and that you would clear the accounts when you returned from Madras.'

My head swam. 'I will see you again,' I said, and went back to the shop.

I once again examined the books. The pages showed a lot of arrears to be collected. Next day I went round to collect all my bills. People looked surprised. 'There must be some mistake. We paid our bills completely a fortnight ago. Otherwise Ramu wouldn't leave us in peace.'

My wife said, 'In your absence he was coming home nearly at twelve every night. He used to tell me that the accounts kept him late. "How was business today?" I unfailingly asked every day. He replied, "Business is good, bad, good and bad. Don't worry. Leave it all to me. I will manage."'

An old man of Lawley Extension asked me, 'Where is that boy you had?'

I told him.

'Look here,' the old man said. 'Keep this to yourself. You remember there lived next door to us those people from Hyderabad?'

'Yes, yes . . .'

'Your boy was gadding about with them a little too much. You know there was a tall, pretty girl with them. Your fellow was taking her out every evening in a taxi. He closed the shop promptly at six in the evening. Those people went back to Hyderabad a few days ago.'

Later on I made inquiries in Market Road and learnt that 75

Ramu had had stitched four tweed suits, eighteen silk shirts and other clothes worth about a hundred rupees, purchased leather suitcases, four pairs of pump shoes, two pairs of velvet slippers, a wrist watch, two rings, a brooch, silk saris, blouse pieces, and so on. I got in touch with a near relative of Ramu's employed in a bank in Madras. I learnt that his old father was hale and hearty, and there was no mention of cholera. Above all, Ramu was never known to have visited Trichinopoly. His whereabouts were unknown. The letter concluded: 'Someone recently returned from a tour mentioned that he thought he caught a glimpse of Ramu in a large gathering during some music festival in Hyderabad. He was, however, not very certain about it . . .'

I sold my shop and everything, paid off my creditors, and left Malgudi. I was a bankrupt, with a wife and four children to support. We moved from place to place, living on the charity of friends, relatives, and unknown people. Sometimes nobody would feed us and we threw ourselves down in a dark corner of some rest-house, and my ragged children cried till sleep overcame them. I needn't weary you with an account of my struggles. It is another story: I must tell you about Ramu. I have to add only this about my own career. Four years later I came across a coffee-estate owner in Mempi Hills, and he gave me a fresh start; and I must say, thanks to him, I have done very well indeed in the coffee trade.

Now about Ramu. A year ago I was panting up the steps of Thirupathi Hills. I had a vow to fulfil at the temple. I had passed two thousand steps when a familiar voice assailed my ears from among the group of mendicants lining the steps. I stopped and turned. And there he was, I could hardly recognize him now. I had seen him off at Malgudi station ten years before. His face was now dark, scarred, and pitted. His eyes were fixed in a gaze. I should have passed him without noticing if he hadn't called out for alms. His voice was still unchanged. I stopped and said, 'Look here.'

'I can't see, I am blind.'

'Who are you? Where do you come from?' I asked in a voice which I tried to disguise with a little gruffness.

'Go, go your way. Why do you want to know all that?' he said.

I had often boasted that if I met him I would break his bones first; but this was not at all how I had hoped to see him again. I felt very confused and unhappy. I dropped a coin on his upraised palm and passed on. But after moving up a few steps I stopped and beckoned to another beggar sitting by his side. He came up. I held up an anna coin before him and said, 'You may have this if you will tell me something about that blind man . . .'

'I know him,' said this beggar, who had no arms. 'We keep together. He has arms, but no eyes; I have eyes, but no arms, and so we find each other helpful. We move about together. He is not a beggar like me, but a *sanyasi*. He came here two years ago. He had once much money in Hyderabad, Delhi, Benares, or somewhere. Smallpox took away his sight. His wife, a bad sort, deserted him. He is vexed with the world. Some pilgrims coming from the North brought him here . . . But, surely you won't tell him I have spoken all this? He becomes wild if those days are mentioned . . .'

I went back to Ramu, stood before him and watched him for a moment. I felt like shouting, 'Ramu, God has punished you enough. Now come with me. Where is your sweetheart? Where is my money? What devil seized you?' But I checked myself. I felt that the greatest kindness I could do him was to leave him alone. I silently placed a rupee on his outstretched palm, and raced up the steps. At the bend I turned my head and had another look at him. And that was the last I saw of him. For when I returned that way four days later, he was not to be seen. Perhaps he had moved on to another place with his armless companion.

# Like the Sun

Truth, Sekhar reflected, is like the sun. I suppose no human being can ever look it straight in the face without blinking or being dazed. He realized that, morning till night, the essence of human relationships consisted in tempering truth so that it might not shock. This day he set apart as a unique day – at least one day in the year we must give and take absolute Truth whatever may happen. Otherwise life is not worth living. The day ahead seemed to him full of possibilities. He told no one of his experiment. It was a quiet resolve, a secret pact between him and eternity.

The very first test came while his wife served him his morning meal. He showed hesitation over a titbit, which she had thought was her culinary masterpiece. She asked, 'Why, isn't it good?' At other times he would have said, considering her feelings in the matter, 'I feel full up, that's all.' But today he said, 'It isn't good. I'm unable to swallow it.' He saw her wince and said to himself, Can't be helped. Truth is like the sun.

His next trial was in the common room when one of his colleagues came up and said, 'Did you hear of the death of so-and-so? Don't you think it a pity?' 'No,' Sekhar answered. 'He was such a fine man –' the other began. But Sekhar cut him short with: 'Far from it. He always struck me as a mean and selfish brute.'

During the last period when he was teaching geography for Third Form A, Sekhar received a note from the headmaster: 'Please see me before you go home.' Sekhar said to himself: it must be about these horrible test papers. A hundred papers in the boys' scrawls; he had shirked this work for weeks, feeling all the time as if a sword were hanging over his head.

The bell rang and the boys burst out of the class.

Sekhar paused for a moment outside the headmaster's room to button up his coat; that was another subject the headmaster always sermonized about.

He stepped in with a very polite 'Good evening, sir'.

The headmaster looked up at him in a very friendly manner and asked, 'Are you free this evening?'

Sekhar replied, 'Just some outing which I have promised the children at home –'

'Well, you can take them out another day. Come home with me now.'

'Oh . . . yes, sir, certainly . . .' And then he added timidly, 'Anything special, sir?'

'Yes,' replied the headmaster, smiling to himself . . . 'You didn't know my weakness for music?'

'Oh, yes, sir . . .'

'I've been learning and practising secretly, and now I want you to hear me this evening. I've engaged a drummer and a violinist to accompany me – this is the first time I'm doing it full-dress and I want your opinion. I know it will be valuable.'

80    Sekhar's taste in music was well known. He was one of the

most dreaded music critics in the town. But he never anticipated his musical inclinations would lead him to this trial . . .
'Rather a surprise for you, isn't it?' asked the headmaster.
'I've spent a fortune on it behind closed doors . . .' They
started for the headmaster's house. 'God hasn't given me a
child, but at least let him not deny me the consolation of
music,' the headmaster said, pathetically, as they walked. He
incessantly chattered about music: how he began one day out
of sheer boredom; how his teacher at first laughed at him,
and then gave him hope; how his ambition in life was to
forget himself in music.

At home the headmaster proved very ingratiating. He sat
Sekhar on a red silk carpet, set before him several dishes of
delicacies, and fussed over him as if he were a son-in-law of
the house. He even said, 'Well, you must listen with a free
mind. Don't worry about these test papers.' He added half
humorously, 'I will give you a week's time.'

'Make it ten days, sir,' Sekhar pleaded.

'All right, granted,' the headmaster said generously. Sekhar
felt really relieved now – he would attack them at the rate of
ten a day and get rid of the nuisance.

The headmaster lighted incense sticks. 'Just to create the
right atmosphere,' he explained. A drummer and a violinist,
already seated on a Rangoon mat, were waiting for him. The
headmaster sat down between them like a professional at a
concert, cleared his throat, and began an *alapana*, and paused
to ask, 'Isn't it good Kalyani?' Sekhar pretended not to have
heard the question. The headmaster went on to sing a full
song composed by Thyagaraja and followed it with two more. 81

All the time the headmaster was singing, Sekhar went on commenting within himself, He croaks like a dozen frogs. He is bellowing like a buffalo. Now he sounds like loose window shutters in a storm.

The incense sticks burnt low. Sekhar's head throbbed with the medley of sounds that had assailed his ear-drums for a couple of hours now. He felt half stupefied. The headmaster had gone nearly hoarse, when he paused to ask, 'Shall I go on?' Sekhar replied, 'Please don't, sir, I think this will do. . . .' The headmaster looked stunned. His face was beaded with perspiration. Sekhar felt the greatest pity for him. But he felt he could not help it. No judge delivering a sentence felt more pained and helpless. Sekhar noticed that the headmaster's wife peeped in from the kitchen, with eager curiosity. The drummer and the violinist put away their burdens with an air of relief. The headmaster removed his spectacles, mopped his brow, and asked, 'Now, come out with your opinion.'

'Can't I give it tomorrow, sir?' Sekhar asked tentatively.

'No. I want it immediately – your frank opinion. Was it good?'

'No, sir . . .' Sekhar replied.

'Oh! . . . Is there any use continuing my lessons?'

'Absolutely none, sir . . .' Sekhar said with his voice trembling. He felt very unhappy that he could not speak more soothingly. Truth, he reflected, required as much strength to give as to receive.

All the way home he felt worried. He felt that his official life was not going to be smooth sailing hereafter. There were questions of increment and confirmation and so on, all depending upon the headmaster's goodwill. All kinds of worries seemed to be in store for him . . . Did not Harischandra lose his throne, wife, child, because he would speak nothing less than the absolute Truth whatever happened?

At home his wife served him with a sullen face. He knew she was still angry with him for his remark of the morning. Two casualties for today, Sekhar said to himself. If I practise it for a week, I don't think I shall have a single friend left.

He received a call from the headmaster in his classroom next day. He went up apprehensively.

'Your suggestion was useful. I have paid off the music master. No one would tell me the truth about my music all these days. Why such antics at my age! Thank you. By the way, what about those test papers?'

'You gave me ten days, sir, for correcting them.'

'Oh, I've reconsidered it. I must positively have them here tomorrow . . .' A hundred papers in a day! That meant all night's sitting up! 'Give me a couple of days, sir . . .'

'No. I must have them tomorrow morning. And remember, every paper must be thoroughly scrutinized.'

'Yes, sir,' Sekhar said, feeling that sitting up all night with a hundred test papers was a small price to pay for the luxury of practising Truth.

# The Evening Gift

He had a most curious occupation in life. Having failed in every effort, he had to accept it with gratitude and enthusiasm; he received thirty rupees a month for it. He lived on fifteen rupees in a cheap hotel, where he was given a sort of bunk in the loft, with rafters touching his head. He saved fifteen rupees for paying off the family loan in the village incurred over his sister's marriage. He added a rupee or two to his income by filling money order forms and postcards for unlettered villagers, whom he met on the post office veranda. But his main work was very odd. His business consisted in keeping a wealthy drunkard company. This wealthy man wanted someone to check his drink after nine in the evening and take him home. Sankar's physique qualified him for this task. 'Don't hesitate to use force on me if necessary,' his employer had told him. But that was never done. Sankar did all that he could by persuasion and it was a quite familiar sight at the Oriental Café Bar – the wrangling going on between the employer and his servant. But Sankar with a margin of five minutes always succeeded in wresting the gentleman from his cups and pushing him into his car. On the following morning he asked: 'What time did we reach home last night?'

'Nine fifteen, sir –'

'Did you have much trouble?'

'No, sir –'

'Nine fifteen! – Very good, very good. I'm glad. On no account should you let me stay on beyond nine, even if I am in company –'

'Yes, sir.'

'You may go now, and be sure to be back in the evening in time –'

That finished his morning duty. He went back to his garret, slept part of the day, loitered about post offices, courts, etc., and returned to work at six o'clock.

'Come on,' said his employer, who waited for him on the veranda, and Sankar got into the front seat of the car and they drove off to the Oriental Café.

Today he was in a depressed state, he felt sick of his profession, the perpetual cajoling and bullying, the company of a drunkard. He nearly made up his mind to throw up this work and go back to the village. A nostalgia for his home and people seized him. 'I don't care what happens, I will get back home and do something else to earn this money.' On top of this mood came a letter from home: 'Send a hundred rupees immediately. Last date for mortgage instalment. Otherwise we shall lose our house –' He was appalled! Where could he find the money? What was the way out? He cursed his lot more than ever. He sat for a long time thinking of a way out. 'Our good old home –! Let it go if it is to go.' It was their last possession in this world. If it went, his mother, brothers, and his little sister would have to wander about without a roof over their heads. But could he find a hundred rupees? What did they mean by putting it off till the last moment? He cursed his lot for being the eldest son of a troubled family. 85

He swung into duty as usual. He held the curtain apart for his master as he entered the cubicle. He pressed a bell. He might be a machine, doing this thing for thirty days in the month for nearly twelve months now. The waiter appeared. No talk was necessary. Sankar nodded. The waiter went away and returned a few minutes later with an unopened flat bottle, a soda, and a glass tumbler; he placed these on the table and withdrew.

'Bring this master a lemon squash,' the gentleman said.

'No, sir –' Sankar would reply; this ritual was repeated every day. Now Sankar's business would be to pour out a measure of drink into the tumbler, push it up, and place the soda near at hand, go out on to the veranda, and read a newspaper there (with the flat bottle in his pocket), and stay there till he was called in again to fill the glass. By about ten to nine the last ounce of drink would be poured out, and Sankar would sit down opposite his master instead of going out to the veranda. This was a sort of warning bell.

'Why do you sit here? Go to the veranda.'

'I like this place, sir, and I will sit here.'

'It is not time for you to come in yet.'

'Just ten minutes more, sir.'

'Nonsense. It is just seven o'clock.'

'About two hours ago –'

'You people seem to turn up the clock just as you like – let me see how much is left in the bottle –'

'Nothing,' Sankar said, holding up the bottle. 'The last drop was poured out.' He held up the bottle and the other became furious at the sight of it. 'I think,' he said with deep suspicion, 'there is some underhand transaction going on – I don't know what you have been doing on the veranda with the bottle –' Sankar learnt not to answer these charges. As the clock struck nine, he tapped the other's shoulder and said, 'Please finish your drink and get up, sir –' 'What do you mean by it? I'm not getting up. Who are you to order me?' Sankar had to be firm.

'Look here, don't you be a fool and imagine I am talking in drink. I am dead sober – leave me alone –'

Sankar persisted.

'I dismiss you today, you are no longer in my service. I don't want a disobedient fool for a companion, get out –' Usually Sankar sat through it without replying, and when the drink was finished he gently pulled the other up and led the way to the car, and the other followed, scowling at him with red eyes and abusing him wildly. Today when his employer said, 'I dismiss you, get out this minute –' Sankar replied, 'How can you dismiss me all of a sudden! Must I starve?'

'No, I will give you four months' salary if you get out this moment.' Sankar thought it over.

'Don't sit there. Make up your mind quickly –' said his master. One hundred and twenty rupees! Twenty rupees more than the debt. He could leave for his village and give the cash personally to his mother, and leave his future to God. He brushed aside this vision, shook his head, and said: 'No, sir. You have got to get up now, sir.' 'Get out of my service –' shouted his master. He rang the bell and shouted for the waiter. 'Get me another –' Sankar protested to the waiter. 'Get out of here –' cried his master. 'You think I'm speaking in drink. I don't want you. I can look after myself. If you don't leave me, I will tell the waiter to neck you out –' Sankar stood baffled. 'Now, young man –' He took out his wallet: 'What is your salary?'

'Thirty rupees, sir.'

'Here's your four months'. Take it and be off. I have some business meeting here, and I will go home just when I like, there is the car.' He held out a hundred-rupee note and two tens. Mortgage instalment. How can I take it? A conflict raged in Sankar's mind, and he finally took the money and said: 'Thank you very much, sir.'

'Don't mention it.'

'You are very kind.'

'Just ordinary duty, that is all. My principle is "Do unto others as you would be done by others" . . . You need not come in the morning. I've no need for you. I had you only as a temporary arrangement – I'll put in a word for you if any friend wants a clerk or something of the sort –'

'Goodbye, sir.'

'Goodbye.' He was gone. The gentleman looked after him with satisfaction, muttering: 'My principle is . . . unto other . . .'

Next morning Sankar went out shopping, purchased bits of silk for his younger sister, a pair of spectacles for his mother, and a few painted tin toys for the child at home. He went to the hotel, looked into the accounts, and settled his month's bill. 'I'm leaving today,' he said. 'I am returning to my village . . .' His heart was all aflame with joy. He paid a rupee to the servant as a tip. He packed up his trunk and bed, took a last look round his garret; he had an unaccountable feeling of sadness at leaving the familiar smoke-stained cell. He was at the bus stand at about eleven in the day. The bus was ready to start. He took his seat. He would be at home at six in the evening. What a surprise for his mother! He would chat all night and tell them about the drunkard . . .

He was shaken out of this reverie. A police inspector standing at the footboard of the bus touched his shoulder and asked:

'Are you Sankar?'

'Yes.'

'Get down and follow me.'

'I am going to my village . . .'

'You can't go now.' The inspector placed the trunk and bed on a coolie's head and they marched to the police station. There Sankar was subjected to much questioning, and his pockets were searched and all his money was taken away by the inspector. The inspector scrutinized the hundred-rupee note and remarked: 'Same number. How did you get this? Be truthful . . .'

Presently the inspector got up and said: 'Follow me to the gentleman's house . . .' Sankar found his employer sitting in a chair on the veranda, with a very tired look on his face. He motioned the inspector to a chair and addressed Sankar in a voice full of sorrow. 'I never knew you were this sort, Sankar. You robbed me when I was not aware of it. If you'd asked me I'd have given you any amount you wanted. Did you have to tie me up and throw me down?' He showed the bruises on his arm. 'In addition to robbing?' Sankar stood aghast. He could hardly speak for trembling. He explained all that had happened in the evening. His master and the police inspector listened in grim silence with obvious scepticism. His master said to the inspector: 'Can you believe anything of what he says?'

'No, sir,' replied the inspector.

'Nor can I. The poor fellow is driven to a corner and is inventing things . . .' He thought for a moment. 'I don't know . . . I think . . . since you have recovered the amount . . . how much did you find with him?'

'About one hundred and ten rupees and some change . . .' said the inspector.

'What happened to the balance?' He turned to Sankar and asked:

'Did you spend it?'

'Yes, I bought some toys and clothes . . .'

'Well, well,' said the gentleman with a flourish. 'Let it go, poor devil: I'm sorry for you. You could have asked me for the money instead of robbing me by force. Do you know where they found me?' he asked, showing the bruises on his elbow. 'Do you know it was nearly next day they took me home? You'd left me unconscious: I will, however, withdraw my complaint. "Do unto others as you would be done by" is my motto. You have served me faithfully all these months . . . but don't come before me again, you are a rogue. Get away now . . .'

'Inspector, after the formalities are over you may send me the seized amount tomorrow, thank you very much . . .'

Sankar starved for two days, and wandered about the street without a place for his head or trunk. At last, loitering near the post office one day, he had a few money orders and postcards to write, which earned him a rupee. With it he ate a meal, and took the bus for his village and back to all the ancient never-ending troubles of his family life.